THE
SILENT
CURSE
III

THE SILENT CURSE III
Cursed to the End

Authored by

ASHLEIGH S. WILKERSON

THIS IS DEDICATED
TO GOD... FOR THE
VISION AND MISSION,

I Thank You.

TABLE OF CONTENTS

ACKNOWLEDGEMENT

To everyone that has gone through something this year but still found a way to smile and push through... This one is for YOU. It seemed impossible, but YOU got it done.

And to each Person that has read and/or supported **The Silent Curse**, **Still Cursing Signed,** **Karma**, **TWELVE**, and is even still reading along with me right now...

YOU are the Bomb and I Love you!

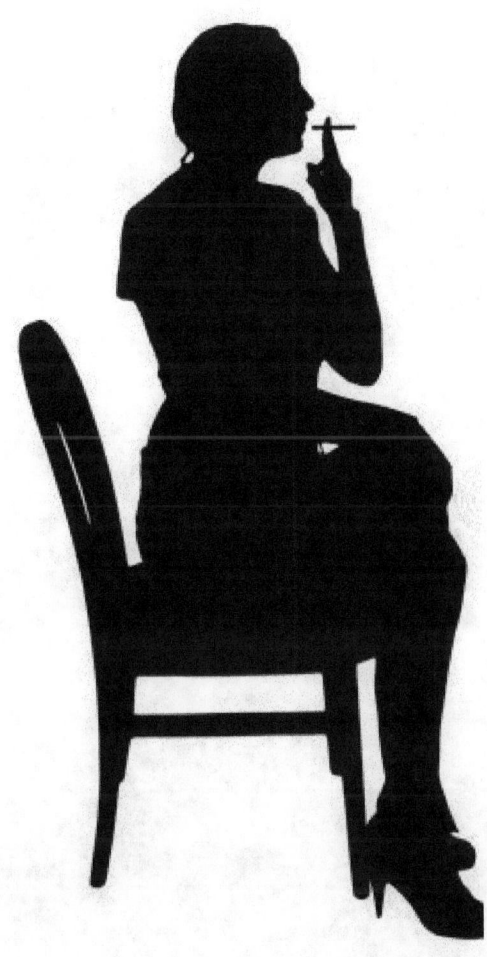

PRELUDE

"Come in and close the door already, you're letting in a draft. Come sit around this table so I can see you. Never liked anyone hovering over me you know that. I can hear your bickering from a mile away. I don't understand why you insist on arguing with these good nurses. Especially the one with the pretty long brown hair, she's still fairly new. She doesn't know much about why I'm here. I've only showed her the same as the others. Of course you'd give her something to question though now wouldn't you? Bet you told her about my parents already. Didn't even know her from a can of paint but you had to release your Pulitzer Prize story. Didn't mention where you come in? No need for a reply because it was a rhetorical question. Of course you didn't. That last episode went much further than planned. I overheard two of the male nurses talking about me as if we'd been acquainted. One actually had a clue. I didn't want to blow our cover so I put on a performance. I looked really spaced out. You know how they expect me to look due to their plethora of non-helpful pills. Yeah, they were actually preparing to give me more and then the younger one that looked like a treat I'd enjoy said the money cleared but too bad what I went through to get it, and too bad I was in there. So being that they are aware, I know that means you are too right? Am I wrong? You don't have to look at the clock. It's only been approximately five minutes since you've sat down. However, I did recognize your new shoes and that fancy blouse. Been shopping lately? I know I made you sound more sophisticated and well off, but the real you could never. So would you like to share anything with me? I prefer to keep an open and honest line of communication. Remember if I ever ask you something, I already know the answer. Which means it would be wise to tell the truth. I like the bracelet too, it brings out your eyes. Are you parched? Would you like some of my water? Well if you're fine I guess I'll tell you what I'm really thinking. I think you're only here because you know that I know you've been given access to my money. Yes, you heard me right... my money. I think it's time that I hop back into the driver's seat. The gossip that's been swarming around the crazy home is that you, Rebecca, and your husband are living your best lives and I am stuck in here looking like a deranged murderer. Now at first I'll agree, I was totally up for the plan. Just for a moment I thought you were different from my parents and your ideas actually seemed logical. But once I realized that Rebecca has no clue, I realized that you're slightly sneakier than I would have hoped. Then again we were still kids, but we're adults now. I'm not oblivious to your evil ways. I'm also great with adding and I know when things just don't equal out what they should. I did not kill my parents. They both died on the inside years ago. But you took care of the actual part. You manipulated the situation and you tugged at my insecurities. And for what? Does cash mean that much to you? Don't you miss your sister? Don't you feel anything? It's been years of you visiting me and I haven't seen not a single tear drop from your eyes. It's rather disturbing if I do say so myself. I wish I were stronger then because I would have told you there was another way. Yes, I'm still trying to forgive her for cheating on my father, but she wasn't always so bad. And my father as well, he had nothing to do with the friction between you all. Yet you killed him as well. You ruined my entire family, and it doesn't even bother you let alone make you feel some sort of remorse. So where am I at now and how do we fix this? Well, I'm not going to beat you up for the past anymore because what's done is done. You're right I did agree to take the blame because I was just a helpless child. I knew this is where I would end up. You didn't put a gun to my head. You only did that to my mama and father. Don't be such a bore it's just a joke. There's no need to be stiff, my conversations aren't even recorded anymore. Check me out, looks like I'm moving on up huh? Did you really think I'd be so sentimental and heartbroken? I mean you still never know who taps in on the audio every now and again. There you go looking at that darn clock again. It's 12:12, do you have somewhere else to be? Or am I starting to slide over the line into your bordered off area? I'm not going to tell on you. I mean it, a promise is a promise. That is my word. Besides, I owe you this. I just want what I'm rightfully owned. Now that I know for sure and it's not an assumption that you didn't have plans of holding up to your end, and you've obviously already irresponsibly spent more than your share... I'd like mine and that's it. See it's that simple. I don't even want an apology or an explanation. I don't want anything but the money that belongs in my account for compromising my freedom for you. I want it, and I want it now! That's it! You can have your reputation, it's not my business what you keep from your husband. Rebecca hasn't seen me in so long that she probably doesn't even remember me. I won't reach out to her either if it makes you happy. I don't even have to stop by your house. I know I'm getting out of here very soon. If you prefer we could meet somewhere, do an exchange, and I could turn my back leaving North Carolina in the dust for good. No more lies or nonsense stories. I don't want anything but a new start. That money would really help you know? Plus, it's what we worked out from the beginning. I know somewhere deep within you that you used to be an honorable woman of your word. I'm hoping by the conclusion of this visit you'll make an effort. We need to find that woman again for both of our sake. Did I say something amusing or flattering rather? Why are you grinning? I'm not being sarcastic or funny. I'm pretty serious. Look I know some things that you went through. I get it, we all have a past. I know my mother made you feel inferior. I know that she was wrong for involving your husband in her scandalous ways. But I also know that she was your sister. It didn't have to be this way especially if you were still going to be with the dog. The truth hurts but there were many more before mama and I wouldn't be surprised how many there are now. No offense but every day we grow older and you can't teach an old dog new tricks. Hell I wouldn't be shocked if he weren't home right now christening that new bed set you got. Oh did you think I didn't know about that? I heard the updated kitchen is to die for. While the story was being told to me I thought literally you just don't know. Anyway, you should have that same energy with him. But you don't, you never did. Why are you clicking that cheap pin? It's starting to irritate my nerves. Or am I irritating yours? Everything I've said to you is just a fact. I'm simply trying to make sure that we have a clear understanding as to my expectations of you within the next few days. Well aren't you going to say anything," asked Mariah?

"I will begin by saying it's good to see you too. You look good girl. Here I am thinking that I've just been called in to make sure you're stable and you're telling me not only are you leaving but you expect some sort of payment from me. Let's cut the sob story about your mother. My sister or not, she was a piece of you know what. She had everything and everyone in her corner. I got one swig of happiness and she just had to gulp it until it was gone. She swiped it right from under me. So before you continue on with this ramble or rant rather, how about you don't and say you did. Your mother and father both got what they deserved. I told your father since before you were born what kind of woman your mother was. She didn't want to be a wife. She didn't even know how too. All she knew how to do was be pretty and take everything from everyone without having to encounter any sort of consequences. No one saw past her beauty. She had everyone in the palm of her hands. When I knew you started to see her for who she really was, I admit I did everything in my power to grasp your attention. I can be truthful and say I even went so far as to use you. You're right I knew you'd end up here too. You weren't an adult. But this was all the court's decision, not mine. But about me? Look at me Mariah. I was too old then so what do you think they would do to me right now? And let's not forget I am her sister. Well they'd give me the greatest sentence possible especially since she used to be involved with the ruling judge. If that isn't ironic. Why do you think his voice cracked a little towards the end of your trial? He's always had a wife, yet he and your mama always had a thing for each other. Do you see what I mean? It had to be done. And we knew that then, so what's the difference now? Is it because you've been here for a lengthy amount of time? Is this place less than the others? Are they mistreating you? Or because I didn't come straight to you as soon as the money was deposited? Yes,

I did purchase one or two things, but how would that look if I came straight here? You have to know that I was on my way. Do you realize $500,000 is a significant amount for any life insurance plan? I know right now you don't want to believe me, but I swear on your mama's grave I did it all for you. Everything was for you. You think I don't know that the money is more yours than it is mine. I know the blood, sweat, and tears that went into what we did. You're going to get it all too when the time is right. Have I ever lied to you before? Now don't go comparing me to anyone else. I'm strictly talking about you and I. Prior to this very moment, have I ever let you down? There's protocol that has to be followed. What we did as you see isn't just something that you get a pat on the wrist for. We're pretty lucky insanity even worked. Some judges would have tried you as an adult. I guess your mama was good for something. Her impression on that judge helped us. If she never did anything else, she helped us that day," said Elaine.

"You must think that I'm that same 16-year-old that you all those years ago. This is so much more than money. This is morality, this is time, and this is justice. Actually I'm having a change of heart. We won't need to meet soon. We can take care of business right now," chuckled Mariah.

"Excuse me? What do you mean? Where is the missing piece? Did they give you a specific date? No one told me anything. I only saw that new little nosy witch up front and she's so ditsy and clueless. So I'm really not so sure that I understand your game," said Elaine.

"I know you don't because you don't listen. But you do speak very well. In fact you speak so well to the point that you've said all the right things. I didn't have a sooner date, well not for sure anyway. But because of this conversation I'm pretty sure I do now. You can come in now Morgan," said Mariah.

"What is that thing on your shirt," asked Elaine?

"Oh you mean the thing that I just spoke into? That's my new microphone Morgan let me borrow for today. She told you she wasn't so familiar with my story right? What she meant was she already knew my story but wanted to hear your side and see which one you chose to stick with during this visit. Isn't that funny. I told her you probably mixed a couple things up but that you'd remember my story for certain. This little gadget is super cool. It really picks up everything. It even records. Isn't that something else," asked Mariah?

"Nope everything she said is just about dead on. I had time today and decided to see for myself. I felt like you left our conversation pretty open. I just knew there was more and wanted to see if I could solve what you believed to be an already solved mystery. Remember you said that just a little while ago," asked Morgan?

"Well isn't this just lovely. I'm guessing you two actually went to school huh? Are you a liar too Morgan," asked Elaine?

"No honey, I'm not like you. Just as I said I heard a little about Mariah. But when she got here, I was intrigued. In many cases patients have very vivid memories and many have very vivid imaginations. Mariah's faked episode was imagination. It was a cover up to protect you, but it was flawed. I could tell something just wasn't adding up so I kept asking her until one day I told her what if I said that I know for sure she was protecting someone. I still didn't have a clue, but she became hysterical. There were water works everywhere. She used at least three boxes of tissues in one sitting. I didn't want to receive that reaction, but from there she couldn't turn back. She thought I knew too much," said Morgan.

"So how did your name become a part of the narrative then? Come on liar let it all out," said Elaine.

"Well you're a little smarter than you look. Maybe we did go to school together when we were little. And did you know that Andrew is my cousin? I actually introduced him to Rebecca. I didn't even realize that she's your daughter. Such a small world right," laughed Morgan.

"You're lying. You're lying about everything. You're just trying to make me say what you wish you had actually recorded. You're as screwed up as she is if you think I'm that dumb. Sugar I'll run circles around you with my project. I am a creator. I can make something out of nothing. That includes people too! You should let her continue on here before you mess around and lose this good day job. I know they're paying you pretty well so you don't need to do anything that could potentially get in the way of your livelihood," said Elaine.

"Do you remember the name of the judge that gave Mariah's verdict," asked Morgan.

"I sure do not. Why would that matter? I know he was scum but that's not even important. Why is he important? What does he have to do with anything all these years later," asked Elaine?

"Fun fact that judge was my Daddy. His name was Morris Garcia. He was not having any sort of relations with Mariah's mama as you'd so like to believe. In fact, my parents were happily divorced when he met Evelyn. He courted her for a few weeks however she informed him that she was unhappily married with a child. It stopped right then and there. He never tried to contact her again. But he never forgot about her either. When he saw you all in court, he said he knew that something really horrifying happened for any of the accusations against Mariah to be true. Since the verdict he'd been fighting behind closed doors trying to save her because he couldn't save her mother. All he needed was a hint or a few details and well it looks like you've given that and so much more," said Morgan.

"This is humiliating. I know what my sister was. I know what she's done to me and so many others," said Elaine.

"Your husband didn't cheat on you with Evelyn. Your husband dated Evelyn first. He told you that it was nothing serious and you decided to walk in her foot steps by dating someone that she was once with. If something happened after that don't you think you sort of asked for it? I've looked into everyone else you've mentioned. No one comes up," said Morgan.

"Not only did you lie to me, but you took something from me that I can never get back. You took my mother, and you took my time," said Mariah.

"So what do you suppose we do now Mariah? You're listening to this woman. Do you even know who she really is? I get it, if it's about finances like I said I just need a little time that's all work with me. I'm going to take real good care of you. Even better than that, I'm going to put you in a position to take the best care of yourself," said Elaine.

"I've worked with you for a long time and it hasn't taken to Aruba yet. I still see signs of Raleigh Everywhere! I have no more time to give to you. In fact, you don't have any more time either," said Mariah.

"Well should I be concerned? Are you two going to kill me or something? I don't fear either of you at all," said Elaine.

"No murder more of an eye for an eye. We'd like you to feel what Mariah has all of these years. It took time for sure, but we finally got you. Once we're done you'll wish your lies were true. Now get in bed it's almost time for your medicine," said Morgan.

"Have you lost your mind? I'm not getting in her bed. I don't belong here. There is nothing wrong with me, and I'm not feeling fatigued. Whether you two want to admit to it or not the whole town of Raleigh and the surrounding area knows that Mariah is delusional. This is her bed. People know me as her aunt. I've been to every hospital she's ever been placed. I promise you won't get away with this," said Elaine.

"You're right, that's too easy. We'll have to move you to another facility. Either way you still have to take this medicine. Let's make it snappy I want to be home around the same time as my Dad to let him know the good news," said Morgan.

"Wait he's in on this absurd idea? How could he? Isn't he supposed to be a judge? A man in a position like his should object. I want to believe you both so badly, but you're both entirely too incompetent and lack the intelligence of a five-year-old. Listen to yourselves. This circus show of yours is going to go up into flames. How do you know that the other facility will work with you? What will you say is wrong with me? How will you explain Mariah going home and me suddenly going to a mental institution when I've been sane since my existence" said Elaine.

"Did you know Rebecca is home? She and Andrew opened up three more stores out this way. She also decided to start volunteering at an institution that just opened up about three months ago. We were going to surprise you when we go there. You seem excited though so surprise Rebecca will be able to care for you and keep you out of harm's way. You've already seen the microphone that Mariah has on, I have one on as well, and Rebecca does too. She's just outside the door right there. Turn around. The entire time you never looked back. You would have seen us at least forty minutes ago," said Morgan.

"How could you Mariah? And to involve Rebecca? She didn't know anything. She didn't need to know anything. I promise I was only watching over you," said Elaine.

"I trusted you. I believed everything you said. My parents are gone and I've

21

spent half of my life stuck in here while you've continued on with life. It's 2016 Elaine! Do you understand that? It hasn't been a year or even two. I've been trapped for well over a decade because of you. The way you're showboating already tells me that if I didn't do my homework you would have booked a one way trip to Cuba and never looked back. I'm not sure if you ever had me in mind but what I know right now is that I have me in mind. Now I'm asking you to listen so that we can all continue to be respectful toward one another," said Mariah.

"Respectful, how is this or anything you all have done "respectful" towards me? How about turning the other cheek? If you're anything like your mama you're God-fearing right? Why can't we pray it out? Why can't you turn the other cheek like I know she would," asked Elaine.

"At one point before the lies that I was fed about my mama, I wanted nothing more than to be just like her. Now I've gained my respect for her again, but I'm going to do what she couldn't. I'm going to let you see how it feels to treat people how you'd never want to be treated. No one ever puts you in your place, Elaine. No one ever tells you that you're wrong. But today is a new day. You are the murderer not me. You wanted them dead...Not me! You didn't even need me if it weren't for the money you wouldn't have suggested forming an alliance at all," said Mariah.

"I'm sorry Mariah. Listen if I could take it all back I really would. I am a person. People make mistakes. You think I don't think about your mom and dad. I know I come off as a strong spirit but I'm not that cold," said Elaine.

"Oh goodness, this is exhausting. Don't lose sight of your dignity. You're

23

almost making us feel bad...just kidding," said Morgan.

"I will yell to the top of my lungs. I will wake up every patient and every nurse and every aid will come storming in," said Elaine.

"I was waiting for you to try that. You always have to be obnoxious. Are you ready for the plot twist? There's no one here but the four of us. Think about it you only really interacted with Morgan right? Did you see the patients get on the busses? You probably didn't even watch. They all headed over to where we are getting ready to ship you. You're totally going to crack up when I tell you this next part. This isn't a crazy house. Nope, it's sure not. This is a recreation center you know... like a big game center. We open it up twice a week to clients from various nursing homes, mental institutions, therapy groups, you name it. That's probably why you confused it as such.

That's also why Mariah wasn't restrained like how she normally is. Does any of this count as a lie or did I still just choose to omit a few minor details? Hmm who knows, either way, I think it's ok right," asked Morgan?

"This really has to be some sort of a bad dream. I think you're both clinically insane," said Elaine.

"Ha, you wish it were, but it is reality mother. It's your reality and it's just getting started. You get what you ask for. I thought I knew you, but I've been floating away in a bubble somewhere," said Rebecca.

"You haven't seen anything yet. You go against me? You choose these filthy broads over your mother? You deny me Rebecca? I made you. I brought you into this world. I'll take you and them too. You mark my words. You all don't know who you're messing with. You all will be sorry, "Elaine.

"I think I've had enough; she's becoming a bore... Rebecca grab her arms. Mariah, you kick her legs from the bag. It's about time she has a seat. We've got stuff to do. This shot to the arm should do the trick for you Elaine. It'll humble you and remind you just how weak you really are behind that ugly mask," said Morgan.

"I swear you're going to regret this. I swear to you, all three of you. I won't be down for long," said Elaine.

"You sure do curse a lot," said Morgan. "She always has," said Rebecca.

"I always will until my end," said Elaine. "We still need you, but maybe in due time if you're lucky. That would probably be better than what you're about to experience now. Then again it is you that we're talking about," said

Mariah. "If you think you're a trip, just imagine the three of us together as one. I hope you're a praying woman like Aunt Evelyn mom because karma always finds its way," said Rebecca.

This is still only the beginning.

CHAPTER 1:
WHERE AM I?

Four twin-sized beds packed into one room sectioned off only by a sheet that wraps around each of their perimeters. Hardly any air circulation most likely due to the aged radiator that keeps singing a flat note. Not too sure what exactly that means, but hopefully it lasts a little longer. There's no sun, just clouds, trees, and discolored grass visible through the rectangular window. Some seats and a table off to the right as well but Elaine doesn't have outside privileges just yet. They say she's a high risk run away possibility. She is never to be left alone. Her pictures in every hallway and bathroom so that the staff makes it their mission to keep her from escaping, hurting herself, or even hurting someone else. Here at Rhythm Fitness Care Center, the patients are first priority. Unlike any other psychiatric center, employees are given three months of extensive training, drills, open door advice, and great benefits that help both them and their loved ones as a thank you for their dedication.

It's still pretty brand new. It was founded toward the end of 2010, just a little over five years by the McDaniel's a young black couple from Queens, New York that relocated down here when they received a healthy inheritance from Sean's mother. She was a ballet dancer and co-owner at Rhythm fit Academy in New York. Yes, the Rhythm fit studio that Debbie Talent always mentions. I know you know Debbie. She's only the best of the best. Well, she taught his mother everything she knows. Sean was her only child, no husband nor father to ever appear. But she made sure that he never needed nor wanted for anything. Avah which is his fiancé, comes from a hardworking middle class family. Her mother was an elementary school teacher for 20 years at various locations before retiring last summer. Her longest stay and furthest commute was to P.S. 149 Sojourner Truth. Her Father whom passed away a little over two years ago was a janitor at the first school her mother worked for. Within two years of dating they married. Her family and friends warmed that they weren't compatible and concerned themselves about her bills and how they would make ends meet. Her mother told them that her bills were her bills with or without the help of her sweetheart. She also told them that sometimes roles reverse and that's okay. She said she saw something in him that she knew was worth the risk. So she worked two jobs to allow him the opportunity to further his education. Once he received his degree they proved all the naysayers wrong. They moved to

Harlem and opened a laundry mat, grocery store, and daycare all located in the same plaza. It was her mother's sacrifices and her father's loyalty that gave her the incentive to follow their footsteps in supporting Sean. And just as a bonus, she and Sean had a little head start because of his mother. The couple are pretty hands on when it comes to all of their businesses. They've learned from the struggles of their parents, which allows them to take multiple trips a year, and afford their employees trips as well. Sean Also guarantees on each application a four-day work week. This means every person either gets a three-day weekend or a third day somewhere throughout the week. Health coverage is free, and all other taxes are at the greatest minimum possible. While growing up Sean remembers hearing his friends that had divorced moms and or single parent homes speaking about their pay, time to rest, and the importance of health care. The way in which their parents set them up has given them the chance to relieve so much stress from the shoulders of current and future employees. Aside from all of that, Sean doesn't believe in hiring anyone that he cannot build with. There are three interviews before a final decision is made. The first is with Avah, the second is with Sean, and the final interview is with Avah's cousin Morgan Garcia. Yes, Morgan and Avah just so happen to be related. Avah's father and Morgan's mother are siblings. Avah also heard all about Mariah's cursed misfortune and wanted to help in any way by providing Elaine with the best service in town. It's been three days since she arrived. Avah was so thrilled to see Rebecca, Mariah, and Morgan that one late evening. She was already hip to the agenda so when Elaine started making up accusations that they were trying to set her up, they went in one ear and right out the other. She never thought to look into things like how long Mariah spent in an institution or how exactly Morgan knew them and why her own daughter didn't feel the need to keep her either. All she knew was that a person was in need of serious attention and she and Sean would be sure to do everything in their power. And that's what they've been doing for almost six whole days now. Sad to say Elaine still isn't used to it. She stands by the window staring for hours chanting you'll be sorry three to four times a day. She barely eats, sleeps, or interacts with anyone. It's 2016 now, one would think she would let it go of whatever Mariah did that set her off so she could get better, but not Elaine. The last thing on her mind is letting anything go. Still with a hint of hope Mariah and the girls called for the best help. They were able to get into contacts with one of Maryland's finest therapist that just so happened to relocate.

"Hello Elaine, how are you today? I'm here with your wonderful new friend. Her name is Tia Andrews. She just graduated with her Masters from the University of Maryland Eastern Shore located in Maryland. Isn't that nice? Different from your last three they were all right from North Carolina. They didn't even make it past day one with your bubbly personality and all. I know coming from out of state that means she has some extra experiences and techniques she's more than willing to share with you. Exciting right? I've told her all about you and she's thrilled to play a part in your progress. This means if you follow through with what's required of you and converse from time to time you may actually get to go for offsite counseling one day. I know you've been through a lot Elaine but I see your growth already and we all would love for you to have a second chance. So don't you want to work with us," asked Avah?

"Interesting, I think you are an incompetent piece of crap. You know for certain what those three did to me. You've kept me here like a caged animal while Mariah the actual murderer and her followers are free. So what would you like me and Ms. Fancy graduate here to talk about? Does she have a solution that guarantees shutting this dump down and imprisoning you all and your system of dense employees? Oh my gosh am I saying too much in front of company," asked Elaine?

"I thought you'd appreciate the act of kindness but I see you do not. We will go now. Maybe another day will be better for you. I'll check back soon. Also let's remember to focus on accountability. Your own actions are what led you here. Remember we always have choice right," asked Avah?

"How about you remember to get out of my room and far from me as possible before I show you something you'll never forget," said Elaine.

"I thought you said she doesn't speak much," said Tia.

"She's just full of surprises today I guess. It's alright we'll leave her for now. Rest up Elaine, but this isn't the end," said Avah. "You're damn right it isn't! In due time you're going to be very sorry you decided to confide in the wrong side," said Elaine. "Elaine it's really enough. No one told you to confess to such heinous crimes. Not only did you exploit your - at the time - teenage niece, but you extinguished your own sister and brother in-law for a hefty insurance prize. Now again why do you think you're in position to analyze anyone?" asked Avah.

"Do you really think she was that naïve? She went along with everything because it was her idea too. Did I get greedy? I sure did. That's what I'm accountable for. But that little prick is a lying coward. She's the one that manipulated my own daughter into conspiring against me. Don't even get me started on Morgan. It was all a set up from the very first moment I walked through the door. They had it all formatted," said Elaine.

"Yes I know; you've been telling me this same story for so long now. Nothing is going to change until you change Elaine. You control your own life. You are in charge of your success and your mistakes. It all comes down to you. It's a shame that you still haven't grasped control of this concept yet. However, until you choose to do so, you will be here. This will remain your home while Mariah, Rebecca, and Morgan are continuing on with their lives. Ask yourself this one question, how often do you think they mention your name? Do you think they talk about you as much as you talk about them," asked Avah?

"You know that only works for actual patients. I mean those that are in here that are really screwed up in the brain. Thanks for the talk but like I said, you're all going to be sorry. Also like you said I haven't been here all that long so whatever brainwashing you've tried, it couldn't have been that much. Don't flatter yourself into thinking that you've shown any form of sincerity. I know they pay you," said Elaine.

"It bruises my heart that you can't feel my genuine concern, but I know when the setting works better for you and you're all good to go you will look back and thank me. You will look back and thank all of us," said Avah.

"No I will look back and laugh at all of you one day as you drown in agony and despair," said Elaine. "You are so creative. The minds capabilities are never-ending. Your hateful wishes are so vivid it's almost terrifying. But it's okay, remember I know what strains you like the back of my hand. No matter how you think you feel about me, I'm still rooting for you," said Avah.

"Well aren't you just a little sweetheart. I think I'm going to vomit. You can let yourself out now," said Elaine.

"It doesn't seem like it right now but everyone means well Elaine. I look forward to our future chats; I know it's going to get better. I know you're going to let me in with time and patience. I can see you're ready to be free of your distress and troubles," said Tia.

"I think you need an eye exam. If that's what you see my dear you're blind. Now please you all are killing me with your ignorance. Go take care of the actual crazies. I'm no longer entertained," said

Elaine. As Avah and Tia walk out of the sliding doors that automatically lock once she swipes her members card through the indigo colored hallway, Avah apologizes for Elaine's demeanor and converses more about Elaine's background. She tells her that she was transported to the institution by her daughter and niece. She tells her that Elaine was basically exposed for framing her niece for the murder of her sister and brother in law. She says that it took just about half of her niece's life and various fabricated stories for her to finally prove what she had been telling nurse after nurse since the day she arrived. As Mariah was switched from place to place, she'd always tell her truth. The story never changed. Elaine on the other hand would fill unsure ears with her side and it would only prolong Mariah's stay. Since she was so young, no one believed her. It only made sense that Elaine would have her best interest at heart while still grieving the loss of her loved ones. Mariah had a history of outbursts so it was a breeze for Elaine to misuse her and abuse the situation. She made up this whole story that portrayed Mariah in a terrible way and then blamed it all on Mariah causing her to look like the delusional one. It was ongoing, and ultimately things exploded. Avah told her it got so ugly because Elaine literally included everyone that Mariah knows in the equation. But she basically gave them different roles and relationships in regards to Mariah. The girls had no choice but to work together in bringing her here. Avah told Tia that the first day she met Elaine she told her that she would be sorry, and then she stopped speaking. Her only way of communicating has been through attacks. She has physically hurt nurses and therapist and mentally scarred a lot of minds. She emphasized her favorite phrase of you will be sorry and told Tia that she hopes she's not easily scared.

While walking past each of the rooms and continuing on about Elaine, Tia notices the faculty lounge. It's so brightly filled with different shades of orange and yellow. Everything matches and has its own place even the remote on the tangerine colored table matches the buttons on the amber colored remote control. Tia stares in awe while peaking her head in for a better look. Avah softly laughs and tells her that they could continue their meeting in there on the sofa if she's comfortable. She says that although her paperwork hasn't been signed entirely, she's a part of the family so it's about time she makes herself at home. Every tooth in Tia's mouth is exposed as she quickly walks toward the chair. Before sitting down on the ginger seat covers she notices the news where she sees three young women emotionally explaining to reporters their worries about Elaine Townsend. Tia looks at Avah and Avah nods her head as if replying yes to whatever Tia is thinking. While placing her fingers on her chin in a worried manner she tells Tia that Elaine must not know that they're friends. They must always remain professional. As time progresses they can express that they've grown closer but Elaine shouldn't think they've had any prior contact let alone an actual friendship. She's really into conspiracy theories. She thinks the whole world is out to get her especially Avah and her husband. She also thinks that Mariah is really the one that should be locked away. She's not ready to own up to anything just yet.

"Would they meet with us? I think if I'm able to connect with Mariah on a deeper level, I could tap into whatever really provoked Elaine. Do you think she would consider the three of us chatting over coffee maybe," asked Tia?

"I think that would be a great idea for the benefit of Elaine. However, this young woman you see has suffered for most of her life. You are still new to town, but word spreads like fire around these parts. Elaine basically made Mariah's parents out to be a freak show. She took Mariah's brain and twisted it in every direction of her liking. This is not a thirty something year old woman you're looking at. On the outside yes, but on the inside there is a child still fighting and until she's ready to address that, she can't help anyone else. She especially won't be able to help the person that created the trauma to begin with. I can ask, but I can't promise anything. If they chose to curse at me I wouldn't even be surprised," said Avah.

"When I was a young girl around the age of 14 to be exact, I suffered from memory loss due to multiple shock episodes. Someone that I called friend and I spent lots of time making memories with completely harmed me. I went days without eating, talking, and rarely closing my eyes because I thought he was going to come back for me to finish what he started. That's what he told me. If I spoke to anyone he would show me the "bad" feeling once more. When I started to talk again and regain my memory, I went to my mama and I told her. I remember she looked me in the face pinched my right cheek, and said well that's what happens when you're not mindful of the company you keep. I was a teenager, still just a girl. But I knew then that no matter how you looked, how you spoke, that no meant no. You know what else I knew or should I say I learned? Sometimes those you love the most, will hurt you the most. Hell they'll hurt you in a way a stranger never could and that's because they really mean something to you. Two years later I graduated high school and made my way to college. I stayed on campus for two semesters while working a full time job and a part time one on weekends. By the end of my first year I got my own apartment. I returned home one time after receiving my bachelors to thank my mother for informing me about the "company" that I keep. Because I walked away from her, I learned how to flourish and to surround myself with people that believe in me, and genuinely love me. You see when a person especially a child or teen openly comes to you and you respond with neglect, they have two choices. The first is to fall in line with what the negative individual is saying or doing. The second choice is to walk away and live the best way that they can. The second way is like a polite form of revenge. You get what I mean? I'm telling you this because although Mariah and I have very different stories, we've both been abused by people we thought we needed the most. However, the person Mariah needs most right now is the person that stares back at her in the mirror every morning. I just want her to know that there is sunshine after the storm and she's not alone. Lastly, when I went home I also told my mother that I forgave her not for her, but I forgave her for me. Mariah needs to forgive Elaine so she can continue on with life without having to feel doubt or guilt," replied Tia.

"I am so sorry that you had to go through that. Oh my goodness I wasn't expecting any of this." Said Avah.

"It's okay, neither was I. There is something about this place. I see something in you Avah that allowed me to step into my vulnerable state. Of course we're really good friends and I think highly of you. But I've never told anyone that story outside the few that knew some years ago. I kind of chose to take that chapter and rip it from my book. You know I give most people the revised and edited version. I never mix personal matters with work related issues, but I just know I could make a great difference here," said Tia.

"I agree. Let me see what I can do about the girls and I will get back to you. For now, I would love for you to really get to know Elaine and see if you can get some sort of actual response out of her," said Avah. "I'm on it boss. She'll be up and socializing in no time," said Tia.

"That's what I love to hear. We really appreciate you and your efforts. I mean it. I'm not just saying it because I have to or because you're a great friend. It means so much having you here with us," said Avah. Avah gently pats Tia on the shoulder as she rises up from the couch. She tells her that she's more than welcome to stay there to work on her notes or watch television. She on the

49

other hand has to return to her desk up front to watch for current and or new patients as well as answer phones. Tia tells her that it's no problem while pressing the recline button on the arm of the chair and kicking off her shoes. She pulls out her gold lap top and starts looking through emails and social media accounts. Then she looks over at the screen again where the reports are still talking about Mariah and her family. She has been reading through every page to the point that she feels like she's personally intertwined with Mariah. She starts thinking about Elaine's side and how Elaine is now where Mariah was. Karma has a funny way of catching up to people at the most perfect moments. She learns about Rebecca, Morgan, Justyce, Andrew and everything else possible associated with Mariah and Elaine. Her jaw can't seem to close. She's flabbergasted that none of her findings are fiction. This is an actual family, and a web filled with horrid tales. It's like something you'd see in a movie but it's real. She continues to flip through the pages a little while longer before a shadow hovers over her side causing her to jump intensely. She looks up to see Elaine smiling down on her. Before she can ask how she managed to get out of her room Elaine tells her she's not necessarily mentally ill so she's able to take advantage here and there as long as she cooperates. Then she asks her if it is okay for her to sit by her and of course Tia tells her sure. Elaine kicks her flat skip shoes off and puts on a pair of light blue socks she happened to have in her pocket. Then she says coffee. Tia is unaware that Elaine requires a cup of coffee before any interaction. She's not supposed to have it of course, but that's the only way to get her talking. Tia thinks for a second if it's best to call Avah and ask permission or to take the moment of vivid information and risk the backlash of Avah at a later time. Before she decides Elaine tells her to follow her. She knows of a more private like room where no one will interrupt them and they won't be at risk of getting caught with her coffee. She also tells her that Avah doesn't really know about the coffee trick because even with two cups of coffee she still wouldn't waste a second of her breath conversing with such a simple woman like Avah. She then smiles and tells her to hurry before they get caught. Tia is already amazed by her dialogue. She can't believe how unaware Avah is. She hesitates knowing that Elaine may be possibly trying to pull a fast one on her, but after reading the reports and records she's so curious to know the juicy gossip. One detail she accidentally left out to Avah is the fact that she's a suspense writer. She knows that documents and or any information pertaining to her clients is confidential but here and there she would change a name or two and that's how she's currently a best-selling author under the Pen name Linda Wryter. Is it slightly sneaky? She doesn't seem to think so since she figures it won't interfere with her work. Nevertheless, she takes Elaine up on her offer as she grabs her things and makes her way toward the door. Before they get completely out, she looks at her one more time as if waiting for a sign of assurance. Elaine smiles and tells her that she promises that she has nothing to worry about. Tia gives a fourth of a grin and the two head for the exit.

This side of the building seems much longer and colder. Elaine isn't really talking again; she just keeps telling her to go straight. Tia finds it weird that the alleged private room is so far, but she's eager for some more girl talk so she just keeps going. There aren't any employees in sight, not one nurse, not even the cleaning ladies. It's still pretty early too.

Everyone can't be on break at the same time. Still, Tia just keeps walking further and further. When she's finally had enough and finds herself getting ready to question the location of the destination, the two arrive.

"Did you remember to bring your member pass from the other room? This spot is a total secret. We can stay as long as we like but once I close the door we won't be able to get back out without your pass. There's also one more area through that tricky hallway that requires it for the way back. Let me know now because if not we can't stay. We'll be stuck," said Elaine.

"Oh, you mean this one? Yes, when I first signed in Avah told me to make sure that I keep it on me at all times. Don't worry, we'll be just fine. You can close the door now," said Tia.

"Awesome, we have just a little over two hours before one of her trolls comes strolling through with that disgusting medicine to put me to sleep. Here you can sit in the blue seat and I'll sit in the orange one. They normally use these for entertainment related activities," said Elaine.

"Thank you, I appreciate it. I'll make sure to have you back in the room before time. This is a very interesting site. In all of my time studying and even during work hours prior to receiving my certificate, I've never been at a facility with a specialized locale such as this. It almost looks like its own separate apartment or something. Does someone sleep here? I know it isn't a conference room, nor another quiet or safe space, but look at the dishes, the stove, sink, table, pictures, television set, even its own bathroom. How exactly did you find out about this little getaway? Have you been here before? Who normally comes here and when? I thought you've only been here for a week? You're sure learning the building quickly," asked Tia?

"Those are all brilliant questions, many of which I had myself. I'm sure you found out a little more about me than I intended you to know through all that biased paper work that Avah printed up. So, you must know that my niece Mariah was here not too long ago. I would visit her very often. I know in the letters and other forms of written documents I'm portrayed as the villain; however, I do love my niece. She loves me too you know? She would confide in me about incidents that occurred here in this establishment and the others in which she was placed. The last time we spoke we had a bit of a quarrel, but nothing too hasty or out of the ordinary. She's still my favorite. She's just a little troubled that's all. And can you blame her? It's really not her fault. She went through so much as a child. Curses doesn't always pass, sometimes it follows you throughout your entire life. I was and still am only trying to help her but being falsely imprisoned in here isn't helping me too much. She doesn't come by, she doesn't write, I haven't heard a peep at all. I'm not pinning any shame on her though. The media, the tabloids, social media outlets, the people in here like Avah and her stupid husband, are all whispering in her ears. She's very impressionable and doesn't know much especially when it comes to stuff like this. She spent almost half of her life in a psychiatric hospital so it's very brand new. I know she didn't mean to do what she did to me. I know she probably feels like crap even on her best of days. I don't hold grudges I forgive her whether she admits to it or not and I mean that seriously," said Elaine.

"It sounds like you've already grown quite a bit since being here.

Honestly I didn't plan to go straight into Mariah's whereabouts but since you've opened the door I will say you all seem rather captivating. I am compelled to listen to any and everything you can give me. I want to help you in any way that I can. But I do need you to understand that we're in this current moment. I know that you have whatever beliefs as to how you got here, but this is and will be the place that you reside until Avah should decide otherwise as a safety precaution not only for others, but yourself as well. Do you know where Mariah is right now? I can tell you that she's safe and living fruitfully. I'm actually scheduled to meet with her next week," said Tia.

"Is that so? Well you can relay a message to her then. Tell her that I love her and I will see her soon. Tell her we are going to work through our issues. We are family, and family must always stick together no matter what. I'm not like everyone else. She and I will always have a bond that no one else understands, and she knows that. So my question is what do you want with me then? What's your greater motive? It can't be to help me because if that's the case what does Mariah have to do with anything," said Elaine.

"I don't know if that's such a great idea. Listen, you all have very different stories as to what happened to her parents and the various other individuals and their roles within your lives. I'm also going to speak with your daughter Rebecca and Morgan Garcia too. They have been keeping in touch with one another. In fact, they've been her greatest support system she says since losing herself. It's always going to be a constant battle for her. Did you know this? Has your daughter come to see you yet? You didn't mention your daughter yet. You haven't been here long at all, she should have stopped by or reached out," said Tia.

"I didn't ask whether or not you thought it would be a good idea," said Elaine. "You're right, but anything pertaining to you seems to be an emotional trigger for Mariah," said Tia.

"As far as my daughter goes, I could care less. She's nothing but a follower. She doesn't know her butt from her head if you ask her. She never did listen to me. She's her father's child. I don't need to see her. I need to reach Mariah. Mariah is the one that could free me from this hell hole," said Elaine.

"The only person that can truly free you from here is you. If you should so cooperate I'm more than sure that Avah would willingly vouch for your progression. You have to learn not to bite the hand that feeds you. Don't allow your pride and anger to block you from your freedom. I do not know most of your journey, but I can tell you don't belong here like the others do. Seems like some misfortunate events came knocking at your door and you opened it up and let them come on in. If there's one piece of advice I'd like to leave you with today, is let go. You have to learn that not everything nor everyone deserves a reaction. Don't allow people to get the best of you. The way you speak and react to people says so much more about your character than theirs. Always think of how you'd like to be remembered. Also sometimes you're going to be the bad guy no matter what decisions you make so just do what's right. I know you're placing a lot on Mariah, but ownership is highly important. Until you see your flaws you will be here while Mariah is out in the real world. Now, you don't have to listen to anything I've just said if you don't want to. However, I'll tell you this. I know Avah a little better than you think, and I know this system like the back of my hand," said Tia. "You're right, and what better way than today to realize my faults. Is it okay if I go to the bathroom really quick? I mean it is right there. I'm sure you trust that I'll be okay right? I'll make you a deal. While I'm in the restroom I'll continue talking to you. But I need to go seriously my guts are bubbling inside. I think it's that medicine. I took it yesterday. It calms my thoughts and helps with sleeping. So what do you say? Do you trust me? The only way to get trust is to give it right," asked Elaine?

"This sounds a little risky. I'm not supposed to let you out of my sight, but it is right there. I can totally see you. I think if you keep your word and speak to me the entire time then it should be okay. Also time check. We've been in this room now for about 45 minutes. Once you're done destroying the toilet I'd say I only need another 15 to 20 minutes and then

I'll walk you back to your room. It's so funny. I was told you don't really talk much at all. I guess you really do have faith in me huh," asked Tia?

"See now that's the spirit. We have to work as a team, it's the only way. You sure you've asked everything? It's true I can go days without any human interaction. I enjoy listening. When you listen you learn things that'll surprise you. Most people only care to talk. On top of that they only care to talk about themselves. That's where they go all wrong. But I do think you're genuine you know. Anyway let's go ahead and make this trip. I know you're going to stand right outside the door. That's okay, I don't even mind. As long as you're okay with a little extra noise pertaining to my stomach then I'm ok. I'm not shy, but I am lactose. The food here really brings out the monster in me," said Elaine.

"You really are sharp. Yes, I'll definitely have to stand by the door. No offense, you've been a pleasure but I still can't take any risk whatsoever. As far as you being lactose, welcome to the club...so am I," Said Tia.

"I get it. Sometimes you only get one shot right? It would be a shame to mess it up. Not every risk needs to be taken. Oh my gosh, looks like we have a dilemma. There's no tissue. Ugh how annoying, we'll have to walk back to the lounge or even my room. I have a roll in my cabinet underneath the sink," said Elaine. "Oh no worry that's not called for. I always keep wipes with me in my bag. Do me a favor I don't feel like walking back to the couch or I'll be tempted to sit back down. I'll stand here by the door and wait for you. Go into my purse in the zipper pocket and get the wipes. You can bring the whole package so that you can take however many you need," said Tia.

"Are you sure? I could really wait here for you to get them. I wouldn't want you to think it's any funny business," said Elaine. "Oh don't be silly. I'm more than sure. Plus, it's literally right there and I can see you from here. I think we've developed somewhat of an understanding. I think you see that I'm here to help you. I know you'll do everything in your power from here on out to make the best decisions. Go ahead and get them," said Tia.

Elaine gives the biggest cheesiest smile as she walks over to Tia's purse. She immediately sees the wipes, and she also sees the membership card needed to cross back to the other side of the building. She also knows it scans the biggest door to exit the entire building. She's not so sure if Tia is aware that she has such knowledge. A little deeper toward the bottom of her bag is a car key with a jeep keychain attached to it. She squeezes them tightly together trying her hardest not to let them jingle. Then she slides them pressed against her wrist into her sleeve all the way up her elbow.

"I got them! At first they fell all the way to the bottom and I couldn't reach. I didn't want to seem rude by turning your bag upside down and throwing everything on the rug. Although as bad as I have to go, that was almost my solution. Thank goodness for small enough hands though. My tiny pinky was able to retrieve it," said Elaine.

"How hilarious is that? I was just about to yell out to you to see if you found them or not. You almost took too long for my liking. But I know the packaging they come in is rather thin. I also have a trillion and one things in that bag. My mother would always ask me what in the world could I possibly have in it. She would ask did I put my whole life in it. Sarcastically I'd reply but of course because you never know what could happen and what you might need in the case of an emergency. It's always better to be safe than sorry don't you agree? So, you name it and I'm sure I have it. But come on and use the bathroom now so we can continue. Time is getting away from us. I do have two more meetings before coming back to you all tomorrow morning," said Tia.

"Oh yes you're absolutely right. Time is so important. I don't think anyone ever takes the time to sit and count the seconds in a day that they waste. They're so used to taking advantage of things like time and opportunities that they never really appreciate the value of having a moment to think, to breathe, or even be free. I know I'm one of those people. Honey I tell you I didn't know what freedom was until I got here. I basically get told when to be alive and when to feel like death all day long with these

67

lame penalties and restrictions. It's all bogus if I do say so myself," said Elaine.

"Now wait a second, don't go backwards. You've been making so much progress. I know we haven't known each other for more than a few hours, but I'm really proud of you. The first step to fixing a problem is admitting to it. Don't run, don't hide, don't be a wuss. I only want to see you progress, so continue to own up to your mishaps," said Tia.

"You're right, I apologize. I get a little carried away when it comes to anything in regards to me being here and or my family and the curse as a whole," said Elaine. "There is no such thing as a curse Elaine. You sound like my great grandparents. I bet you believe in those old spirituals our ancestors supposedly sang as well," asked Tia?

"Child I think you should be careful disrespecting those before your time. Curses and hymns are very much a thing.

Do you know anything about your culture," asked Elaine?

"I know your beliefs are what got you here so if that's what you're believing in, I'm going to pass. Now please hurry. We need to conclude this session. You're taking away from your own time. I know you don't want to be back in that bed but at this rate you'll be there sooner than later," said Tia. "My beliefs have nothing to do with anything. Hold on a second. Let me release this here gas and soon as I finish we'll resume. I really don't like verbalizing much but if you think you have this mess figured out child you're sadly mistaken. A person that doesn't believe in no one is a person that can't do nothing for me. Why you ask? Well with a mind like that you can't do anything for yourself so you definitely can't do anything for someone else. But I wish you were right. This curse round my family for years. My relatives have been hurting one another left and right like a contest. Not one wanted to admit to their wrongs, so it just keeps going and going," said Elaine.

"Now see that's what I mean. That's that spirit talk again. How about some individuals in your family made bad choices? The results of those choices hurt others within the family and caused a chain reaction to follow. But, if someone down the line chose or even chooses now to do or be different than the example before them, then a different outcome would occur. Which means there's no curse, just a line of selfish people following in the footsteps of other selfish relatives. Now go ahead, the minutes are still ticking," said Tia.

"I beg to differ. But you're right we could go on and on but the clock won't stop so I'll just go on in here and make it quick so we can get back to it. We never know what the day still may bring. I'm really glad to have you here with me that much I can tell you for sure," said Elaine.

As Elaine locks the door, the lights start to flicker as if the bulbs about to blow. She starts counting backwards from ten and tapping her foot gently against the wall. Tia requests that she stops making any sounds and focuses on using the bathroom. She tells her she thinks one of her biggest issues is her level of concentration. She tells her the first place they need to really zone in on is her focus outside of her situation and her family. She gives a complete diagnosis, multiple solutions, and a variety of possible scenarios should Elaine cooperate but receives no feedback whatsoever. She taps at the door and calls out to Elaine but she still refuses to respond. She figures something must have aggravated her stomach, that she really needs to sit on the toilet. The clock is still ticking and it's now almost 5:30 p.m. so their session is over. The few minutes they did have are out the window now so all she has to do is walk her back to her bedroom and make her way to her vehicle. She picks up her purse and digs in the pocket for a stick of gum and her keys. The gum comes out without a problem, but the keys aren't in any of the sections within the purse. With one hand she flips the bag while screaming for Elaine at the same time. Still, Elaine says nothing. Tia jumps up and rushes over to the bathroom door banging on it again and it opens effortlessly. As she peeks her head in calling for Elaine in a much softer tone, she notices the lights are off, the seat hasn't been sat on, and Elaine is nowhere to be found. She steps in while looking back making sure that the door hasn't closed. She softly calls her name three more times before the door shuts and locks behind her. She immediately turns around to reach for the knob when she hears Elaine begin to laugh. For a second she thinks what a relief. She feels like Elaine is being harmless and accidentally locked the door behind her. She thinks Elaine is hiding somewhere in the bathroom with her. Now she definitely believes there's something mentally wrong with Elaine and that she's just being a typical patient. She's excited because she really wants to help her. The lights start to flicker again, but she still can't see Elaine. She calls out to her four more times but Elaine refuses to say or do anything. An evil chuckle comes again before she tells her that she's on the opposite side of the door with her keys in her hand. Tia gasps while trying not to. She politely asks Elaine to open the door explaining that she wouldn't be in any trouble for the cynical prank and she'd still receive her last few minutes of open conversation.

"It's a crying shame that you don't look to a being higher than yourself. If you did you would have seen this coming. You really let me go in your pocketbook and into the bathroom by myself. Lord have mercy you must have received your degree yesterday. I mean luckily there isn't anything wrong with me but there is definitely something wrong with you. You lack intelligence. You lack common sense especially in this field. You're a tool! Honestly you should be in my seat and I should be in yours. Honey you're better off working with the kids. No that's not true, I'd pity the person willing to leave their most prized possession with you. This was easy as pie. Truth be told it was almost too easy. That concerns me. So let me tell you what's going to happen from here. You're going to stay in this bathroom until one of the cleaning ladies should come. The crazy thing is this wing is specifically for attendees that fail to cooperate. Most times they're sent this way for a day or two with total supervision. When I say total, I mean they can't even switch cushions on the sofa that's how closely they're watched. I guess I could have informed you. But then again you'd already know if you were doing your job correctly. Moving on, if one of the ladies should come that means they were actually doing their job. That's the other thing if there's no patient scheduled for this area, they won't always do the extra cleaning and checking up. Oh and one more thing once I pull down the second door that you probably didn't even notice, the room will be sound proof. That means you can scream until your heart is content but unless there's a good reason they won't go the extra mile to raise the door. Which means I'll have more than enough time to leave you here and do whatever else I need to break free from this garbage piece of junk center. Don't feel obligated to respond the second door is halfway down so I can't hear you already. Don't worry it won't be more than a few days I'm sure and you'll be freed. The great news is so will I. It's tough I know. I should have been a comedian. I mean I doubt you'll ever be taken seriously again and lose all credibility but then again who needs a job right? You're young, you're pretty if all else feels be a social media model or a blogger of some sort you can still give just as much advice and tips. See there's always a plus side to things... Anyway I must be going now. Don't bother to look for your purse or anything. I have everything you need with me. I'll enjoy our new jeep too. It's crazy I've always wanted a jeep especially a white one like yours. Mhmm, I saw the cute little emblem. I love the color. I'm going to name it Nino White. What do you think? Ah, it doesn't even matter because it's all mine now. Well, I hope you enjoy your stay. Take care...and the moral of today's session is maybe if you listened to our ancestors a little better you'd know when God is sending you a sign. I bet you wouldn't be trapped in the restroom of a crazy house. I enjoyed our time, take care and be blessed child. I've got a curse to attend to," said Elaine.

Tia pounds at the door while chanting various explicit words. Elaine doesn't hear any of them. She's just laughing and using Tia's lip gloss and putting on her shades, fancy hat, and cardigan. She's ready to exit. She does an extra look around the room making sure that she has everything she needs before giving the knob a good turn.

"Is this some sort of a corny joke? Why isn't this door opening? Hello is someone out there? You've got to be kidding me. Why can't things ever flow peacefully? What did you do? Very clever Tia. Alright, I'm going to open the doors just so you can help me escape. If you try any funny business It'll be the last thing

77

you do. Do you hear me? Well not like you can talk back just yet but I'll repeat the rules for you once the first door is lifted," said Elaine.

Elaine walks back toward the sofa placing the purse and keys down. Then she bends over to drag the first door. It's heavy and made of great quality so it's not sliding as it should. She calls out to Tia but she doesn't answer. She figures she most likely has an attitude so she continues opening the second door. Once unlocked the door sways back and Elaine walks in to see that Tia isn't there. She's not in the room at all. Suddenly the lights start to flicker again and a voice comes on over the loud speaker.

"I have to let you know that you had me going for just a couple of seconds. I didn't think they would allow such treatment. There had to be another way out. I thought they were being too strict on you, but now I see everyone is right.

You are right where you need to be. By the way I hope you enjoyed all of my props. I love the car name, but my actual jeep is Black. It's kind of gross you'd wear my lip gloss, and thank God we don't have the same ancestors because yours let you down today sugar. Now I'm going to give you back the blessing you threw at me. I insist you enjoy, we'll talk soon I'm sure," said Tia.

"You can't do this to me child. Let me out of here. I swear I'll hunt you down," said Elaine.

"That doesn't sound like a God fearing woman to me Elaine. I was in your corner but you found me to be helpless. You thought you had another fool to bamboozle. But I'm off the clock now and I have more than enough time to stoop to your level. I'm not sure who exactly is telling the truth as to why you're here, but you should know on your end that it's not looking so peachy. Now don't make

79

threats you won't live up to. The nurses will see you in the morning," said Tia.

"You tricked me. You didn't come here to help. You wanted me to react," replied Elaine. "No what did we say about being liable? You reacted because you wanted to and the way in which you chose to behave is because that's who you really are and how you felt. Don't be a victim honey," yelled Tia. "I will show you a victim in due time and that's law," said Elaine. "Wade in the water... wade in the water... children wade in the water... *God's gonna trouble in the water*," said Tia.

CHAPTER 2:
THIS SESSION WILL BE DIFFERENT

The sun barely shows up as November starts to glide away. Dead is the way most things look and seem... Two weeks went by without Elaine muttering a sound. She refuses to eat or see anyone. It's not like she has a million and one relatives or friends hoping for a visit, but Avah thought she'd at least consider speaking to the local reporters and supporters of her tragic case. However, she turns them away just the same.

She was given an old wooden rocking chair. It's broken to the point that one side leans a little but it moves and grooves still. For hours she sits by the window staring out toward the grass and rocking back and forth screeching and blinking every so often. The only time she interacts is when it's time to receive her medication. A woman that only cared to take her daily vitamins, she now takes about three different pills. The doctor believes she's in a state of shock but he has hope for her. He thinks it's beneficial for her to stay for as long as she needs. He thinks she's way out of touch with the outside world. Things like cell phones, laptops, even forms of transportation and certain foods may seem pretty foreign by the time she's free to go home so he wants to work with her as much as he can to create an easier transition for whenever that day should come.

Mariah hasn't called or visited. But Tia comes twice a week. Even after their first dispute, she knows in her heart that she can bring Elaine some sort of tranquility. She tells Avah to try reaching out to Mariah again. Avah obeys but returns with the same insignificant information. She has no reply from Mariah, not an update, not a text, a recent post on any of her social media platforms, not anything at all. Tia bows her head in disappointment and tells Elaine that she thinks she may have another way to get through to her. Before fully learning of her plan Avah tells Tia no matter how bizarre of the suggestion to go ahead and do as she pleases. She explains that her idea is more than what she has come up with, that she is desperate at this point, and really just wants some sort of remorse from Elaine. Tia comforts Avah by reminding her that Elaine isn't as bad as she thinks and that she's dealt with a woman that burned her family's house down killing everyone in their sleep. Then when she was brought in to get help she spoke with a shrink as well and wrote a book in which she brought everyone back to life. Her reason for murdering her relatives was because she wanted more privacy. She asked her parents to take an all paid trip on her and they refused. Her

Dad was a surgeon and her Mother was a pediatrician. Both jobs are fairly demanding and the couple always booked vacations responsibly and when they felt they both could equally benefit. How can you enjoy vacation knowing you have so much work to do? How can you take pleasure in knowing that your team may be drowning? These are the things both parents considered. She didn't see it that way. She believed her parents were choosing their careers and wants over hers. For a long time, she felt unloved and like she didn't matter. As she grew older the roles reversed and she felt they no longer mattered. She wanted to be left alone except she couldn't afford to move out. Anyway, once she was taken in because of course she wasn't in the home during the fire, she became mute. It took months and months until a colleague offered Extra Help Practices. Extra Help Practices is a company located twenty minutes from here. They're actually all over from Maryland, Virginia, even Atlanta. Their mission is to connect with inpatients on a deeper level. They try to explore risky patterns and behaviors. For example, when abusers are younger just like anyone else they may have dolls, kitchen sets, cars, and other similar toys. "Have you ever offered a child a doll or a car to play with and watched their idea of "playing"? Now, imagine this experiment using real people and objects," said Tia. Avah looks lost of course thinking that if the young woman killed her family she can't possibly mean ghost. She's also not too sure about what real life objects could help her deranged state of mind. Tia tells her it's no ritual or haunted scary practices. She tells her that the company has trained personnel that know how to tap into a place that no matter how hard professionals try, they just can't. Avah raises an eyebrow out of curiosity and Tia tells her that if she's ready to have an open mind that she can show her better than she can tell her. She says she has a friend in the car that will only come in if she sees fit. She explains that this small yet powerful ally was able to break down the woman that killed her family in the burning fire. She states that not only did the woman admit to everything, she's now an advocate for others going through similar family issues. She tries to convince units to come together and communicate about their difficulties rather than look to violence especially to the extent that she did. Not only has she said sorry, she now wishes she would have done things differently and she's able to comprehend the severity of her irrational decision. Avah is astonished. Tia can tell so she asks her what her company has to lose. She tells her that technological advances, safety measures, and the will to make a difference should be her greatest worries but above all else to heal people like Elaine from the inside out. She firmly explains that that's her greatest concern and that she wouldn't do anything to put Elaine, nor the reputation of the company at risk.

"Alright, I guess you've convinced me. So where is this secret weapon of yours and how does it work," asked Avah.

"I've just sent the ok. Go open the door. You all should meet at the same time," replied Tia. "Is it some sort of package, or a drink? How does it work? I'm not understanding the real life connection here," said Avah. "As soon as you answer the door, you will understand. Just remember to keep an open mind. Be thoughtful of the things you say or feel because energy can be transferred," said Tia. "Are we talking about an object or a person here? I think you're beginning to lose me again," said Avah.

"This is a practice that I know everyone will benefit from. You want answers right?

Mariah wants answers right? Elaine hopes for freedom as well? Does her family or what's left of it prays for serenity? Trust this technique and I can almost guarantee you all will walk away as winners. Now hurry I've received an alert. Our little gift is here," said Tia.

Avah makes it through the building almost to the lobby doors before hearing the bell ring. As she pulls the handle, she greeted by the happiest face of a little girl no older than 10. She looks at the child as if waiting for her to ask a question when she notices the child hasn't blinked or moved from that spot. Then she sees a tag around her neck that has a list of instructions on the back. Avah tries to pick the little girl up without making a spectacle of herself, but she's terribly heavy. She puts her down while wondering where does she store her weight because she looks and seems so tiny. Before trying to move her again, she takes out her phone and texts Tia to come to the front. Moments later Tia is standing before Avah smiling as if it were Christmas.

"At first I thought she was a child; she looks like it. Her lifelike features are superb. The creator is very talented. I've seen dolls like her but her height and weight and even her hair and ears all seem too real. Then, I caught her flaws. Her smile remained and her eyes have yet to blink. The instructions manual shocked me the most. Am I missing something? Are you suggesting a doll that almost looks and seems too real has and will help women like Elaine?" said Avah.

"It sounds to me like that mind is closing up by the seconds. First off you didn't finish reading the instructions or you would have discovered her name. Avah I'd like you to meet Kennedy Davenport. Before I go further, you really need to get with the times. It's 2016 you as a business woman should have already heard about the Davenport experiment. Kennedy although one of a kind, has four siblings. They are each designed to fulfill certain expectations. They all contribute to different senses and fields," said Tia.

"So not only does the doll have a full name, but she has siblings too? Do you hear what you're saying right now? How am I supposed to take her seriously?" asked Avah.

"You should take me seriously because as of right now I'm your best bet. I've been watching the news. Poor Mariah the kid caught a tough break. The whole family failed her. It's a shame you know? As for Elaine, she's a horrible person but very smart. I would love to go deeper into her mind to see how in the world she thinks she deserves anyone's sympathy. People like her take advantage of people like you all. That won't happen with me. Also don't call me a doll ever again. That's like me saying you didn't accomplish much because your husband was already loaded. Now is that a fact? Eh it depends on how you look at things right? I'm not a doll darling but you're right I'm a little less than an actual person I guess. See again it depends on how you look at things? It's kind of like the glass half empty or full right," asked Kennedy?

"Did you hit a switch or something? How did she do that? I know it wasn't really her just speaking to me. Cut it out Tia. I get it I lied a little bit about Elaine's background but this isn't funny," said Avah. "There is no lie. Did you see me touch her," asked Tia?

"Yeah what are you talking about? Tia doesn't control me. I'm my own person...don't be a wise girl either. You know what I mean. I'm Kennedy, a genius girl in disguise. I was created to help you. Now stop being a donkey and show me to our girl already," said Kennedy.

"But how is this even possible? How are you speaking right now? If no one turned you on how are you speaking to us," asked Avah.

"You sure do ask a lot of unnecessary questions. I'd hate to be your husband. Talk about an annoying nag. How does your cell phone track you? How do you get all the news and weather without watching television? Do you own one of those tablet things that looks just like your phone? Do you know a thing about smart devices?" asked Kennedy.

"Is it safe to say that you're being the wise girl now," asked Avah.

"It's safe to say that technology is a powerful thing and that is how I am possible. Now show me the way. We don't have all day you know. I'm not free. What most charge for an hour, I charge for a half hour," said Kennedy.

"Tia I'm still waiting for you to say that this is all a gag or something. We're not really going to allow a doll to talk to Elaine. I think your other patient was delirious. Maybe she was incredibly sick or in denial or experiencing symptoms of anything other than what Elaine is going through. She will immediately hop into defense mode and think that we're trying to make a mockery of her. The last thing I want is to make things harder. Like our little friend said she chargers by the minute so when she goes home or wherever we're supposed to send her, we'll be left here fighting with Elaine," said Avah.

"That's the thing, she's not going anywhere for as long as we need. Also you'll be amazed at what she's capable of. How about we give it a try. Let's take her in to see Elaine. We should watch her. If she indulges, we'll allow things to continue to see if anything will happen. If she totally disregards her and us as well I will say you were right and Kennedy will leave. It's as simple as that. Kennedy looks like a child no matter how you feel about her. People love children. On top of that since she's not really a kid she knows how to say and do things that will help Elaine get to a place of acceptance. We both saw from my initial sit down with her to even the last few, she still thinks she's done no wrong. We need her to work on owning up to her mistakes. What do you say," asked Tia.

"Ok. I'm going to say I don't think it will help, but I doubt that it will really hurt either. We'll try it your way. Plus, you're right. If there are any serious complications Kennedy can be sent back to the lab she came from. What's the worst that can happen," asked Avah?

"Splendid! So we're good to go then. But one last thing. Before we introduce the two, I'd still like to have a conversation with Mariah. I know she has to be curious about her aunt's status," said Tia.

"I thought you moved past it. Listen honey I'm telling you this isn't a good idea. I haven't even heard from Mariah. Don't you think the girl deserves some freedom and a chance at a normal life? She's in her thirties for crying out loud," said Avah. "I reckon you're right, but I also reckon you could be wrong. Who said I'm looking to stir up some trouble? I know what I'm doing," said Tia.

"No, you think you know. Some things are better off being left alone. I mean truthfully tell me what is your obsession with this poor girl? I've already agreed to your bizarre practices and theories so what else do you want? Like all things aside I put my name on the line because we're supposed to be friends. Or does that not factor into the equation at all? Did you forget or am I missing something? I just don't get it. Why is

97

disturbing Mariah so significant to you," asked Avah?

"I never ask nor question you about your profession. You asked me to come here remember? You said I would be the one to get the job done. So I'm here, and I'm working on the task at hand. Friends don't block each other from advancing and being great. There's a method for sure but nothing devious. Why are you interfering," asked Tia?

"I wouldn't say that. I know you are an expert, and I'm not saying this because of who you are to me. You're hands down the best. However, either you care too much or you care just enough for a reason outside of the patient. Is there something else you're working on? Is Elaine contributing to another project?" asked Avah?

Before Tia gets to rudely respond, the lights start to flicker. The first time they go out everyone is sitting right in their rooms and the hallway as they were before the glitch began. The second time,

Tia notices she can no longer see Kennedy. Avah starts hollering in laughter because she thinks Tia is playing a joke on her, but Tia's face is flushed as if she'd seen a ghost. She immediately pulls her hair back into a bun, places her things down on the chair and tells Avah they should try and find Kennedy as quickly as they can. She tells Avah that she hadn't placed the batteries in Kennedy just yet. Avah's smirk dies and the frown that appeared could take a person's soul if it tried. Tia digs the batteries out of her back pocket proving that the doll indeed has a mind of her own. Avah slaps her hand across her forehead and pulls out her phone to call her husband. Tia tells her to put it away and assures her that they have everything under control. Avah gives her an annoyed face while screaming how can things be under control when a toy doll with no batteries is somehow walking around a mental facility. Both girls are panicking. The bickering is off the charts, and every insult there is has been named at least seven times. In between curses Tia tells her that she isn't just a doll and that's probably the reason why she chose to show her what she's made of. Avah isn't amused. She tells Tia that if they don't find Kennedy that they will both be called insane. She tells her no one else would have allowed her idea to begin with and if she makes her look bad their friendship and partnership will be over for good. Tia tells her to simmer down, that she's being extreme, and needs to take a load off. The lights flicker again, and there is Kennedy sitting in the chair next to Avah's belongings. She looks at Tia in total disbelief. She blinks really hard and the lights flicker again. This time once they flash back on Kennedy and Tia are both nowhere to be found. Back and forth the building goes from pitch black to light, the faucet starts to drip, the floor creeks, and the door knob turns back and forth. Cold air feels the atmosphere, and not a single voice in the whole facility makes a sound. The lavender walls are sweating, the room is closing in, and Avah sees everything she and her husband built quickly being yanked right from under her. She starts walking from room to room grabbing the handles and calling names that choose not to respond in return. Each bed lay empty. Not an article of clothing in the drawers, closets or even on the bed. The entire facility is vacant or so Avah thinks. Suddenly the room is in flames from the amount of body heat swarming around Avah. She reaches for her bag to buzz the security alarm but of course it's no longer there... as if it disappeared in thin air. The entire purse, her coat, everything is gone. The lights turn back on and she calls for Tia but instead she finds Kennedy sitting back on the loveseat. She stares the doll down for thirty seconds. As her eyes blink she's blindfolded from behind and forced in a seat against her will. Frightened and confused is what she is. With little to no hope left, she decides to give Kennedy a chance and cries out for her. She feels foolish, crazy, childish, plain old dumb, because she's just a man-made human like figure, but right now she's desperate. Anything is better than being stuck in a room full of crazy patients that actually can't stand your guts and hate everything about your existence. Some of the residents had the privilege to return to the real world but when visited by the state and asked multiple questions, the final question was asked to Avah. She always felt no matter who it was, they weren't ready yet. She wanted to guarantee a full recovery so she always denied their growth ending in a rejection from the state. She wanted to extend the payments she receives per person. Guess you can see why she doesn't have many fans here.

"Hello…Kennedy are you there? Listen I feel like a moron. Don't believe me to be ignorant, I'm aware that you're a piece of plastic. I know we're into the future now, but you're not a person. People don't have battery packs. How exactly you're speaking without it being loaded is another mystery I'd like to solve. If you'd be so kind, I would totally appreciate it. Can you hear me? Where are you? I know you were just there a few moments ago. Have you seen Tia? Is she okay? We were talking and then I was grabbed from behind. I can't even lie I'm a bit confused. There's just so much going on."

A door slams shut, one light comes on, and Avah sees that her company is no longer in the room with her. She wipes her eyes a little harder and she suddenly disappears from the room. In fact, not only is she out of the area, but she's no longer located at the care center at all. Instead, she's in a house. It's unfamiliar but she could tell that it's been abandoned and lifeless for some time.

"Hello? Is anyone home? Kennedy are you here? I think it's been more than enough time now. I'd like to go home. My husband should be getting off soon. I know he's waiting on supper. He's such a hard worker. He's probably worried sick about me. Tia are you here? I get it, you really want to speak with Mariah. Fine, I'll make a phone call. I still can't give you a yes for sure, but I can try. Why are you ignoring me? Come on, I feel like I'm talking to myself. I think I'm ready for supper too. It feels like my stomach is about to explode. You'd think it's been much longer than a few hours. Can you tell me what time it is? Also can I use your phone? I'm not sure where any of my stuff went, but I really need to call my husband."

Avah rambles on for about ten more minutes or so before receiving a flyer beneath the door. On it she sees a picture of her and a date. In parenthesis it says missing three weeks, a reward, and a phone number to call. The name belonging to the number is none other than Tia. "What is this? Am I supposed to crack up or throw something? Tia what is going on? Are you there? Whoever you are I'm not missing you imbecile. You don't know who you're dealing with. Do you hear me? Do I make myself clear? Let me out of here. I demand you let me out right now," screamed Avah.

"And what if I choose not to," replied a faint voice.

"Tia is that you? Show your face, you dweeb. You have the nerve to take me from my place of business and my husband for hours, show yourself," said Avah. "It's been way longer than that honey. Your establishment and your husband are both fine. They're not missing you," said the voice.

"And what is that supposed to mean? When are you going to tell me who you are? What's with that bogus missing picture, and when will I be returned," asked Avah.

For someone that's not calling all of the shots, you sure do have a lot of questions. How about you shut up already and let me continue taking the lead. I mean it's not like you have much of a choice anyway. So, sit tight... we're just getting started. From here on out I'm asking all the questions. Do you follow," asked the voice? "How do you expect me to have any sort of a conversation with you when I don't even know your name? What do you want? Is it money? I have lots of it. I can give you any amount, any object, anything you'd like," said Avah.

"Well that was fast. Not too long ago you called me plastic and now you're ready to turn over your savings. Look at how the tables turn. I don't want your money girl. Besides as loaded as you are, you can't afford me. Do you know who I am now?"

"That's impossible. Where is Tia? That's the only way. You're a doll," said Avah.

"Looks like you're still a tad bit under the influence. I told her those drugs weren't strong enough. I'm not a doll or a robot. That was a skit we performed to keep you off our heels. I've always been able to speak because I don't require batteries you fool. I'm a person just like you. I'm thirteen years old and Tia is my cousin," said Kennedy.

"I'm beginning to feel like I'm in the twilight zone. None of this makes sense," said Avah.

"Okay let me break it down a little further for you. Elaine is Tia's Godmother. I bet you didn't know that. Ha, some friends you two are. Anyway, Tia is writing a book on psychological family trauma. Tia wanted to speak with Mariah without compromising her position at your company so she and Elaine decided to keep their relationship away from you. You also denied Tia access multiple times in regards to speaking with Mariah. So we brought you here for a while so that Tia could reach out without any complications," said Kennedy.

"I'm still stuck at the fact that you're a real little girl now. Do you realize they're using you? You're not even old enough to understand the things that that wicked family has struggled with. Things so bad that you don't even need to know. I didn't even want to know. It's a part of my job and any decent human wouldn't want to keep opening an old wound. Mariah suffered enough. She didn't want to speak with Elaine. She didn't want to speak about her either. Your cousin is a user and an abuser. Information between her and any person that sits in her seat is supposed to be confidential. I knew she seemed too eager. All of this for a book? You do know this is kidnaping. Where is my phone? You can break free right now if you call Sean, my husband and tell him where we are. You are a child. They know better. They did to you the same thing that Elaine did to Mariah. They are manipulating you. Why else would they tell you to pretend to be a toy. Do you see the extreme measures they went through in order to pull off this scheme? You have your whole life and so much potential. I can see it. Don't be like them. Tia was brilliant and I say was because when my lawyer finds lout about this, she won't work anywhere ever again. As for her book maybe being behind bars will add an extra spin on things. It might actually sell," said Avah.

"You're upset because you fell for a talking doll? And I don't plan on going to jail but I think you're right, that could spice things up a bit. Think about it a shrink and an author. I believe you're just bitter that I'm brilliant. But it's okay I'll be sure to give you an honorable mention. Thanks to you I'm already half way there to winning my Pulitzer Prize. I can hear them already...and the winner is Tia Andrews. My name has always had such a ring to it if I do say so myself. What do you think? Hell it really doesn't matter. Sorry for being so blunt but it's the truth," said Tia.

"And after you receive your award and everything else that you have in mind, what happens then? What are you going to do with me? Should I just sit back and watch you all profit from another young girl's misfortune," asked Avah.

"It all depends on you. You can choose to be a team player or you can choose to be in my way. But I should warn you that if you work against me, you've chosen to be in my way. I don't think that's a really good idea. You were kind of on your way there before and look where that got you. Before I came down here, my book was already more than 80 percent complete. I needed that one on one with Mariah and look, a masterpiece is on the way. I know this is going to be a bestseller. I can feel it in my toes. I have something here for certain that is going to make my readers go nuts. So with that being said, once my manuscript is approved I'll let you go. When my book comes out should you decide to speak to the blogs and whoever else, you'll look sad and mad. You might even look a little crazy depending on how I decide to bite back. But right now I can't risk it. I'm almost at the end. You see what I mean," asked Avah.

"I think you're sick. I'm not sure how you're supposed to help others. Who would want to use someone else's pain for profit? As soon as I get away from your delusional self, I'm reporting you to every website and social media outlet there is. I might even create one myself. I don't know what happened to you but you're not the same sorority Tia I once knew. Those words we vowed to live by mean nothing to you. Where did your morals and integrity go? Did you ever have any? Was it all just a mask? I really can't believe this. Next thing I know you'll be saying something ridiculous like you brought Elaine along for the ride or something," said Avah. "And why would that be such a bad idea? Looks like we underestimated you," said Elaine.

"What are you doing here?" asked Avah.

"I'm here for the same reason as you Avah. Didn't you want me to open up to Tia? So what is troubling you now? I've come to realize you stir up altercations but run just as soon as it gets too close for comfort. We figured meeting in a setting like this, you have no choice but to sit here and listen to the way in which you've meddled in the lives of others," said Elaine. "I've done no such thing. I am only doing my job. That's all I have ever done. Are you not listening to Tia? Did you hear her say that she's also an author? She is trying to exploit you. She's not taking notes, she's building a novel and you and Mariah are the leading ladies. Doesn't that bother you? Don't you feel used? I hired her to break through your tough shell. You're comprised of various layers and I had a moment of desperation. She's impressive, phenomenal, brilliant, absolutely intelligent, and dominates in the world of psychology. But this is abuse of power. I was wrong and my judgment of her is very off. If I knew she were working on a narrative other than encouraging and helping clients, I would have never called her here. I mean that. I'm serious Elaine," said Avah.

"I don't have to believe a darn thing you say. Honestly I never have since the day you trapped me in the hogwash facility of yours. You knew then, and you know now that there is nothing wrong with me. But just like she wants exposure, so do you. You treat me like a piece of art opening the door to every Tom, Dick, and Harry that nudges you for a chance to speak with me about my niece. Not once have you ever asked me if I were up to it. Do you know why? No, you don't know why. Well I'll tell you. It's because you could care less. As long as you're making money who cares if my name is being thrown out the window," said Elaine.

"I've never said that. Of course I care," said Avah.

"You didn't have to. Your actions show it all. And yes you do care only about yourself though," said Elaine.

"It looks like you all have two different perceptions of me. I see your intentions for what they are. But she doesn't believe you because you're the one that's been dishonest with her," said Tia.

"You just shut up. No one asked you anything. You won't get away with this. Mariah won't have anything to do with you," said Avah.

"There's nothing to get away with. All I needed was a few conversations and well that's been done. Looks like you don't know Mariah as well as you thought either," said Tia.

"You lying sack of…"

"Now, now... please be careful. I wouldn't want you to say something you can't take back Miss Perfect. But I'll go ahead and enlighten you just a bit. Over the past two weeks, Mariah and I have had brunch and dinner at various locations. I told her that I knew Morgan, Rebecca, and you of course, very well. She didn't fact check me at all. I guess your reputable names were more than enough. Instantly she took me all the way back to her childhood to the tragedies in which she was falsely accused. There's so much devastation there that I don't even know where to begin. She's so timid at times and assertive at others. It's like her body has a natural timer for looking a person in the eyes. A few seconds and her attention would always shift to her napkin or her blouse. She also places her hands over her face a lot as if she's trying to block something out. For a woman of her circumstances, she looks absolutely amazing. I would have never thought that she would be in her thirties. She looks much younger, around 21 maybe. I guess that's good karma for her. Ah now did I make a funny? You know since your karma isn't so great. That was childish I apologize. How dare I pick at you while you're down? That's not so fair of me," said Tia.

"You are a bastard. You are a conniving and despicable woman. I don't know how nor do I know when but just as soon as I am free of you, everyone from Maryland to Atlanta, to California, to Japan, will know what you've done. I pray for the sake of your career in all aspects that it was worth it," said Avah.

"Child I don't need your prayers. If anyone needs prayer right now, it's you. Calling me names won't settle anything. Do you think this is the first time I've had an angry broad like you jump down my throat? I advise you to get a clue you stupid prick," said Tia.

117

"Guess you're familiar with a few names yourself huh? I'm not going to continue stooping to your level. I'm just disappointed that a woman of your credentials would jeopardize it all. Come on T, you've worked at General Hospital. That's one of the best companies in all of Maryland. Do you really want to throw your future away for a possibility at a best-selling book? You're not even sure that it's going to succeed in the market. You can stop this right now. I won't hold anything against you. I'll go back to minding my business and write you a letter of recommendation for anywhere you'd like. I figure too much has happened for us to continue but I still want to help you. I know deep down you're just lost at this second. You've gotten caught up in the hoopla of this Mariah madness. It can be fascinating especially if you're not from around here. But I've actually studied Elaine and Mariah thoroughly so I know she toyed with you. It's all a façade. It's okay to be defeated by Elaine. It happens to everyone at some point. But I am telling you that there's still time for you to move on from this. I want to help you. I'm still your friend. We are a part of the same sisterhood," said Avah.

"I'm more than well aware of where I've worked. Since you know it all I've actually worked at Raritan Bay and JFK too. None of that matters. Right now I know what my art can become. You're not an artsy-fartsy kind of girl. You're the type of person that always has to have a set plan and do everything by the book. If you lived on the edge once in a while maybe you would have seen all of this coming. Or maybe you'd be more of a risk-taker. My degree will always be my degree. I will have it to fall back on no matter what. I'm not worried about you or anyone else when it comes to what I've worked for. Do you see the difference between you and me? Your one-track mind will prevent you from achieving so many things. Like for instance that fine husband of yours. I bet if you gave him a little more attention than your work, you all would be in a better space as well. And I know you're sitting there thinking how can I possibly know about your marital problems? Well, he's been confiding in me for a little over six months. What can I say, I needed to know you a little better too. And who better than your husband to help me? It just so happens we shop at the same sneaker store. I needed shoes for the gym one day and he was there. Do you know he actually spoke first? Not anything out of the ordinary a simple hello and a smile. I knew from there your tall handsome man in the Nike suit would cooperate with almost any subject I felt the need to bring up. No doubt about it I had him in the bag. Luckily for you, I'm not into married men but I'll tell you one thing for sure you better start snatching his eye back because if I were… well, I won't even go there. Plus I know how that feels so I would never. He did take the hint and remained grounded in your vows," said Tia.

"I know my husband he prefers a Mercedes, not a Buick. Let's leave him out of this. Since you're trying to play unfair you can disregard everything I've said as far as furthering your career. I'll leave your next destination up to you. All I will continue to reiterate is that following the lead of Elaine will end in disaster. It is detrimental to your future and I know for sure you will lose everything. No one is going to care about all the good you've done as a licensed therapist, author, or whatever other title if you're acting out of character and being unprofessional with clients like Elaine," said Avah.

"You really make me sound like some sort of monster. I'm not all that bad. You're being rather biased," said Elaine.

"You don't have to be in denial. It's ok to look as long as you don't touch. That's all we both did. Thought I'd be a sister and let you know that," said Tia.

"It's enough from both of you already. I'm done, what do you want from me then," asked Avah.

"Finally, we thought you'd never ask," said Elaine. "So here's the thing, as mentioned, I've had the pleasure of conversing on more than a few occasions with Mariah. I've done my part in making her feel comfortable. I've provided her with clarity and perspectives outside of her own when considering her family's curse. I think she has shown a lot of effort. But Elaine wants a chance to speak with her alone. I agree with this talk because it's real dialogue that I can take from to include in my literature. So, where do you come in? We want you to convince Mariah to come to Rhythm Fitness Center to have an in-depth one on one discussion with Elaine. We also want her to agree to hear and openly accept Elaine's apology. I want her permission to quote all of her comments verbatim," said Tia. "So you want me to help you all further make a spectacle of this young woman's misfortunes? When is she going to live her life without constantly being reminded of her dysfunctional relatives like you? As for you, Tia are you insane? Why would you allow her to suck you into this? I don't even know what to say to you," said Avah.

"We're not asking for all of your opinions. This is what is needed from you. So now you're left with a choice," said Elaine.

"Marvelous, so it's easy... I won't have anything to do with this. You know that this woman cannot stand to be in your presence for more than obvious reasons. So why would I orchestrate a gathering between the two of you? It's clear as day the choice I'm making," said Avah.

"I figured you wouldn't comply so easily. You're right, your choice is clear. But I don't think when given a choice we were so clear. I was hoping you'd be able to make it without any force, but I guess I was wrong," said Tia. "Are you getting at something? How do you suppose you're going to force me?" asked Avah.

"Your husband is very faithful. He is so successful; He's worked hard to provide you all with such a wonderful life. Someone like yourself having to work from the bottom up, I know you must appreciate it," said Tia.

"This is the second and last time that you're going to refer to my husband. I'm thrilled you find him attractive you skank, but as you've said multiple times, he is already spoken for by me, of course," said Avah. "You're right, he is spoken for," said Tia.

"Okay then, so let's find a way to come to an agreement that doesn't pertain to him," said Avah.

"But who speaks for you," asked Tia?

"Excuse me? What are you asking me, Tia?" asked Avah. "It seems like you're a little agitated. Is everything okay," asked Elaine? "I'm fine just trying to understand what the two of you are trying to pull," said Avah.

"Here's the thing Avah, we're not trying to pull anything. We are not accusing you or that amazing husband of yours of anything," said Tia. "Well, isn't that reassuring not like there would be anything anyway. As you said, you guys exchanged a look and a hello. There is no harm in a greeting. My husband is a nice man, but I know he isn't the friendliest. I'm secure within my marriage. No offense, you're beautiful, but you're not his type. We have endless love, that R&B

kind of love. That's something you can't come in between," said Avah.

"You're right. He's not friendly. I guess I bent the truth some. I did try him and he passed. He told me that he's happily married. He also said I'm pretty but what he has with his wife surpasses any physical attribute possible. I remember thinking to myself wow what a man. Only a real genuine person obligated and devoted would walk away from the meal I was trying to serve him. But that's the difference between the two of you. You, on the other hand, you're friendly and you did allow someone to sip your shake if you know what I mean," said Tia.

"What are you talking about," asked Avah? "Oh, would you cut the act already. The two of you are killing me the way she's allowing you to drag this out. So let me break it down in simpler terms for you. She is saying that we have been following you and your drama just as long as you all have been following me and my niece. Yes, you can close your mouth now. I know it's totally wild. But yes, we know that you've been cheating on that almost perfect partner of yours with not only another man but his close friend Trevor Neverson. Now please spare us all by not lying. We have both visual and audio evidence. We also have a written statement from the hotel manager. What can I say he also found me to be pretty? We went on two dates and I saw footage of you both coming and going to the same room. I saw you guys holding hands down the hall too. Must I say with everything you have to lose, you're not much smarter than I am, huh? My, oh my, … but don't worry. Here's where things get perfect and start to work in your favor. We don't want anything but what we've asked you for," said Tia.

"So I don't have a choice? You two are trying to blackmail me? So what happens if I still decline? What happens if I actually come clean to my husband?

"In a perfect world you'd be an honorable dummy. Either way your intellect must have been hidden in your purse when you decided to step out on him. But again we all know he carries you. You also know that should you tell him about this affair he's going to leave you and take every single dime with him. With his reputation you won't get anything. Looks like the bottom is looking pretty near again to me," said Elaine.

"You don't know anything about me and my relationship," said Avah.

"I know that unlike you he is insecure. Guess I hid just a little more truth from you. He thinks with work he hasn't been performing in all areas as well as he could. Don't worry I assured him that he's a great guy and his wonderful wife that would be you Avah, is more than lucky to have him. Look at that I am a good friend to you," said Tia.

"We are not friends. You worked for me and that's it. I'm warning you to leave him out of this," screamed Avah.

"I'm not sure how I feel about your tone. However, I won't let it cloud my thoughts if you should make the best choice for everyone and that's to cooperate," said Tia. "So what now? I guess I'm between a rock and a hard place right. I'm sure there's a bug somewhere in here. What do you two want from me," asked Avah.

"That's a girl! Ok, first we'll catch you up on the dates I've had with Mariah. This may take a while. You may have to call your sweetie and inform that you'll be a little late. After that, we need you to call Mariah and tell her that she has to come to the center. You will tell her that you suggest she and Elaine release the negative tension between them. You will tell her that it will enhance her growth and that it is in her best interest to join in on this sit-down," said Tia.

"This woman is a trigger for her. Why can't you just speak to them separately? You're not thinking at all. Please, I'm humbly begging you to consider going through with this idea. I'm sure the last time they spoke, Mariah said everything that she ever wanted to say to her," said Avah.

"Did you consider undressing for Trevor or how did that come about? I'm just curious. Poor Sean, I know he'd be crushed to know someone else saw what belongs to him," said Elaine.

"You are everything Mariah says you are. I don't blame her for hating the air that you breathe. No matter what you've never amounted to anything close to her mother. That's what it is. You're still trying to fill a void. She wants nothing to do with you. She knows and sees you for who you really are. No therapy session is going to change her mind," said Avah.

"Yeah well these photos of you and Trevor may change your love bugs. So are you ready for Tia to begin now," laughed Elaine?

"You're so disrespectful and no matter what scheme you come up with she's still going to look at you as she already does. There are just some things you can't come back from. I don't know if you know but no one wants to spend more than half of their life in a mental home. What you took from her, no amount of money can ever buy. But go ahead, be my guest. Let's hear about these noteworthy sessions Tia. I'm eager to know what has made you so obsessed to go so far as to ruin my committed marriage. You think it's ok to sit here and judge me? Every relationship has its ups and downs. I love my man. This is really low of you. Can't say Elaine blew my mind but I thought I knew you," said Avah.

"Honey you are the one that cheated. I don't understand how. Many people would kill for what you have. Everyone always wants more or different I guess. I'd call that ungrateful. What do you think? Why can't people be satisfied? Nevertheless, things are a little more than bumpy. Couples normally talk things out before falling in the lap of someone else. Isn't there supposed to be some kind of chemistry between you? Maybe a level of understanding? Unless you decided to skip that step altogether. I can't really be too sure. Infidelity is not something you can flip. If you're wrong, then you're wrong. In this case, you're wrong. Am I'm just as devious for blackmailing you? I guess one could say so, but if you were living a life of a married woman, there wouldn't have been any dirt for me or anyone else to uncover. So who is to blame now you or me? Don't worry you don't have to answer that. Right now you can let me do all the talking. Just make sure you have on your listening ears for when I decide to test you. I'm telling you this is good stuff. Once Mariah and Elaine get to have their podcast moment I'll be able to include all of this in my book. I'm seriously excited. I couldn't have done any of this without your help. I get it right now things aren't as you'd hope for but thanks to you some good is going to actually come from all of this. This story is going to take me to my greatest height thus far. I can feel it," said Tia.

CHAPTER 3:
TIA WANTS TO MEET MARIAH

Tia and Elaine pick Avah up by her arms to stand her to her feet. Tia grabs her keys and the three ladies head for the exit. Tia tells them it would be a good idea to go over what happened during her sessions with Mariah at her house. It's "Whip It Up Wednesday" for her which means she has to cook up a mixture of items that she already has in her home. She tells the ladies that she'd love to give them a meal and a coffee or beverage of some sort while they go over the details. Avah isn't so thrilled but seeing that she doesn't have much say-so she nods her head and asks if she is able to speak with Sean first. Elaine tells her that she's fair and doesn't see the harm in her telling her husband that she is taking part in a sleepover. Avah looks at Tia almost for a sign of confirmation. She's not so excited to spend the night anywhere with the two of them but Tia agrees with Elaine and tells her to let her significant other know that she'll be home sometime tomorrow afternoon. On any other regular day they would speak at least two to three times so he was already missing her. During the car ride she sat in the back seat with Elaine so there was only so much privacy. She was behind Tia's seat and Elaine sat directly in the middle almost on her lap. That's how close they were. Avah is so overwhelmed she begins to stutter. She's trying to think of a lie suitable enough to capture her husband's attention from her staying the night out. So she finally comes up with needing a little girl time. She tells him how she hasn't been out in a while and needs to spend some time with her girlfriends. She tells him that she's going to be with Tia and another girlfriend from her sorority. She knows if she mentions Elaine at all it'll be a red flag for sure. He'd probably leave work just to find her. On top of that if Elaine's dark brown eyes could kill her they would without a second thought. She hasn't closed them not once for the sake of assuring that Avah doesn't try any funny business. Sean finally says he's okay with her staying but tells her to be safe and make sure that she locks her doors. There have been multiple break-ins in the neighborhood over the past few weeks. Little does he know her car is at the facility. But it's not like she's going to need it anyway. Full of shock and stress she forgets to mention that part, but she does say that she'll be careful. She also says as soon as she leaves there tomorrow she'll head straight home. He jokingly checks the time telling her it's already past noon so he hopes the rest of the day flies by. Tia mocks her sobbing while nudging her to hurry things along. Elaine's devil like laugh echoes throughout the room. Both women yell for her once more by saying that she's about to miss the best part of the thriller. Avah tells Sean that no matter what she loves him so much. He chuckles and tells her of course and how he can't wait to have her in his arms again. She hangs up and immediately Tia grabs her shoulder and brings her into her living room. She shakes her head in disappointment telling her how dumb she is to have ever put their relationship at risk. Avah tells her to mind her business and start her confessional already. Elaine lets out a hysterical yell. Tia isn't so amused as she slaps Avah in her face. Avah takes it and releases a smirk as if to question her strength. Tia raises her hand again but Elaine intervenes by blocking the smack. Then she looks at her to remind her of the reason they're having this intimate powwow. Tia takes a big gulp to swallow her pride and sits down next to Avah. She pulls back her hair, kicks off her shoes, places her phone down on the coffee table, turns her television down to a whisper, and slides back in her seat. She seems to be rather comfortable. Elaine follows stepping out of her orthopedic crock like slippers. Then she pulls her wig off. Avah is surprised to see the long hair that drops from under her short wig. It falls down her back and slightly curls at the end. Before she can ask about it Elaine tells her she's always worn wigs as a way to protect her natural hair from being damaged. For that quick second they shared an understanding. Avah was still amazed at her hair but she could totally relate being that her own hair is always in a different style and or color. Tia rolls her eyes and tells Elaine to stay focused. Elaine snaps out of Avah's compliments and puts her lengthy hair in a slick bun. Then she looks at Tia and tells her to resume. Tia places her hands together and places them in her lap. Then she tells Avah that she and Mariah met in total, five different times in five different settings. Avah's left eyebrow quickly raises. Tia explains that she knows it's not proper protocol but she knew that if she asked, she would say no. Avah says then doesn't that mean it's probably not a great idea. Tia raises her eyebrow in return and tells her not to worry about good and bad ideas unless she's talking about the one that involves sleeping with a man other than her husband. She says that's the only bad idea she should have acknowledged. Avah chokes to hold in her cry. Elaine tells her she'll be fine as long as she does what is asked of her. Tia shows no sympathy. She tells them that there are so many women killing themselves to be perfect in hopes of finding what she has and she doesn't even appreciate it. Elaine agrees but reminds Tia at the same time that they're not here to give her new found integrity. They've taken her by force to explain why she should convince Mariah to sit down and speak with Elaine for the final time about their family's murder spree. Ultimately this has nothing to do with Avah, or her husband. She's just the middle man needed to bring everyone together. Tia agrees yet again. Then before getting into things she feels the sudden urge to make herself a snack. She gets up and walks into her golden orange and royal blue kitchen which is inspired by her favorite basketball team, the Knicks, and pulls a microwave package of popcorn from the top cabinet. She tells Elaine to watch it while she goes to the bathroom. You can hear her singing songs at the top of her lungs. Avah takes this as an opportunity to breakthrough Elaine. Avah begs her to let her go. She tells her she won't even go to the authorities should she let her go and return to the facility herself by tomorrow evening. Elaine thinks she's a riot and a real character. She tells her that she can't be serious. She says what would be the logic in returning to a mental institution when there is nothing wrong with her mind. Avah says that may be true but until proven otherwise she's supposed to be there. She also says she can see that she doesn't need to so she will do everything in her power to help. Elaine calls her a liar and tells her she's just like a lawyer or a politician giving her hope but knowing in the end things may not go as stated. She wants a definite outcome and knows that Avah can't guarantee anything other than locking her away for years and years. The toilet flushes and out comes Tia. She suspiciously stares at Avah and back at Elaine. Neither of the ladies say anything as Elaine grabs the popcorn from the microwave and makes her way back in the living room to join the party. She tells Tia that the floor is hers. Tia turns the brighter light on and begins to run away with the events revolving around her encounters with Ms. Beauvoir.

"The first time I met Mariah was two weeks ago. Before moving down here I already knew I wanted to speak with her. Actually if I'm being honest, she's the only reason I agreed to come and work for you with such short notice. The money is great but I was doing just fine where I was. But I knew with my income from you all plus my earnings from my soon to be Pulitzer, I'd be quite well off. Anyway I don't want to get off topic. Then again it's not like you have somewhere else to be. Ha I sleigh me. But seriously, the internet is a remarkable source. I was able to research all of you. Do you know that for a fee of just $40 you can find out almost any piece of information on a person? Isn't that terrifying? For example I found your mother's resume and a picture of her and her first boyfriend. That's also how I was able to hack your lover boys' phone records. I'm not sure that it's so smart of you two to have so many texts and photos of each other. I'm just saying right now your Sean doesn't have a reason to suspect anything of you, but one day he might grow curious and actually look through your things. Once you get into your phone it's pretty self-explanatory from there. But back to the topic of the hour. We met at the gym. I read somewhere in a broadcasted interview that she loves working out, planting flowers, and baking. I'm not a flower girl at all, nor do I like to bake, so that meant I had to make my way to the gym. I'm more than aware to what meets the eye I seem to look physically put together. However, that elliptical almost took me straight to heaven. Although a little terrified, that's what actually helped me. She noticed that I was having a hard time and she gave me a few pointers. It was a simple friendly 101 gym course that lasted all of two minutes, but tit was pleasant. Then, when I was leaving I decided to use the bathroom which is located in the locker-room. She noticed me and asked how I was feeling. I replied pretty sore, but in a good way. She followed up with the old gym cliché no pain no gain and we shared a smile. After I came out the bathroom I saw her gathering her belongings. She had this really big tote bag that was stuffed to capacity. I was curious so I asked her if she was going far away. I'm sure I was obvious as my eyes kept staring at the luggage size purse. She closed her locker, put her boots on, her jacket, and a black cap. It was a little windy so she was pretty prepared. Ten, she finally responded to me. Once a week she meets with her therapist. At this point she didn't go too far into the curse, her parents, or even Elaine. She said she doesn't have a lot of family and friends that she feels comfortable with confiding in so she searched high and low for the best Doctor in town. I thought right then and there oh this has to be fate. What are the odds? She needs someone to talk to and here I am. To me that meant her current Doctor had to vanish. That way I could show her how much I can be there for her. Please don't stare at me like that. I didn't do anything drastic or out of the ordinary. I'm just a woman that knows and goes after what she wants. I want this story. My theme is all picked out. I know how everything is going to play out down to the exact ending. Does that make me a criminal? I don't think so. So, I convinced her to sit down with me that very day. She canceled with her shrink and we went two blocks from the gym over on Wilkerson Blvd to grab salads and sandwiches from Quick Eleven. You know the little convenient one stop shop. They have a really nice little dine in section now. So once we got our food we sat down and hopped right into it. I believe we were there for three hours before her phone rang. It was the voice of a man. She became so silly like a little school girl. I could see she was happy and maybe even in love. Before the call ended she made sure to say I love you Trevor. Mhmm what a plot twist right! Your little fling and her loving boyfriend have the same name. At first I thought so too but Raleigh isn't all that big. What's the coincidence? So do you know what I found out then? I'll tell you. I found out that he's the same Trevor. I also found out that you knew. Please don't put on the confused face. We both know I'm right. I tell you hackers make things almost impossible to get away with. Here you were telling me and Elaine about sparing her from more pain and you're having an affair with her current boyfriend. Next time don't send messages to Trevor bad mouthing her. You never know who may get ahold of your text messages. See, I'm trying to help you. I mean it's too late this time but once a cheater always a cheater. I'm sure you'll sacrifice poor Sean again one day. Nevertheless I'm not putting on a guilt parade not right now anyway. You know what you did, and you have to eat sleep and work with that on your mind. Although I bet it's much harder knowing that it's not such a secret since we know now. All in all that's still not the point. I apologize for the tangent. So after her call ended with Trevor, she and I kept talking about her aunt Elaine for the most part. She really broke her heart. Which I have to say surprises me Elaine because you're so sweet. But things happen right? No one is perfect. We can only continue trying. It had to have been late in the afternoon almost evening when she finally got up to head home. She said she had an interview in the morning and wanted to make a good impression. We exchanged numbers and made arrangements to meet the day after the following at 2p.m. on Princeton Place. There's a bowling alley I was dying to check out. I figured might as well have fun while building my manuscript. Before I continue, are you thirsty or anything? I don't want to seem like a bad host. Like I said this may take a little while. I want you to feel at ease. It sounds like crickets. Well ok then but you can't say I didn't offer. We met up the second time. We both are terrible bowlers but we enjoyed the chicken tenders and French fries. I mean who doesn't? Isn't that like the number one go to meal when you're going out to eat? We talked a lot about her parents and her biggest fears. Every time an old song came on she was reminded of her mother. Her eyes would get watery but she kept bowling. This is also where I met Trevor too. Oh yes, your love interest stopped by with some pretty red roses and a kiss on the cheek. Isn't he sweet? I almost thought so too. They shared their stories about how they first met and shortly after he left us to finish bowling. He said he had something to finish up at the office. I wonder now if that something was you. Don't worry I won't make you answer. That's none of my business. That time didn't last as long as the first. I needed to seem like I have a life too. So I told her I was having a dinner at my cousins and needed to be home soon to prepare. The great thing is I could tell I was making progress with her already. I could tell she enjoys my company especially since she invited me to her bible study class for the following Tuesday evening. Jesus is indeed my homeboy so I figured sure why not. Bible study is normally an hour or so right? Child I was wrong and totally in over my head. Do you know we were there for four and a half hours? You know the church right? Mount Zion on Bramhall Avenue. You have to know it. Trevor goes there too of course. What a coincidence the moral less boo practices the word. I hope that didn't come off the way I meant it. I'm sure it did though. By the time we finished the class, she was drowning in a pool of tears. She couldn't stop the waterworks. She said she felt so free and like she really knew herself for the first time in her entire life. I was curious what scripture gave her such clarity. I wanted that feeling too, but I didn't want to be too pushy. She's so gentle, so kind and modest. She's nothing like what I assumed. The media portrays her a very assertive woman, and that's not the case at all. She's so soft spoken. I had to ask her how did she gain such strength and during that class she told me by coming here. She said her faith gave her something no one can ever take again. She said the word of God allowed her to forgive every person that has ever wronged her and to really open her mind, heart, and soul to receiving love. Do you know who else gave her a little motivation? I bet you do...that's right Mr. Trevor Neverson. Did you know that he's an usher at the church? Or did I just tell you? If he wasn't hugging and tugging you on the side, he'd sure be a great catch. But we all have flaws huh? After that meeting, we agreed to do brunch at the Twelve Seasons over on Convery. It was a chilly day. Do you remember Joseph Morehouse from LMN News 13 said we were getting snow flurries? Child all of Raleigh was in an uproar. We didn't get anything but a gust a wind but it was chilly enough for a coat. All we both ordered was soup and hot tea. Do you know she's not that much older than us? Do you know she considers you her friend? Now if I'm correct a friend wouldn't sleep with your boyfriend. A friend wouldn't lie to you, and a friend sure wouldn't use your name and agony nor exploit you in hopes of furthering their businesses and brands. I think she uses the word friend a little too loosely when speaking of you. You are not her friend at all. Do you even feel bad? Do you think about how she's going to feel if and when she does find out about you and Trevor? I mean I'm still thinking about poor Sean. Neither of you are worth anything. How do you have such genuine people in your lives. The last time we met was two days ago. We had brunch again but this time over on Hall Ave. She told me that she decided to leave her shrink. She said she feels more at home speaking with and spending time with me. Do you know how that made me feel? Can you say confident?. At first I really just wanted to pick her brain, but as time progressed we really have become friends. Don't get me wrong I still have my agenda just as Elaine does but she's really a wonderful soul. During this intervention she showed me a floor plan. She said she had the chance to tour three different houses and she was planning to purchase one at the end of the week. My next thought was Trevor. She literally read my mind. She said that they are becoming even more serious and they want to live in the home together. I wanted to be happy for her. I really did, but I could only think about you two. Don't worry I still haven't said anything yet. We spent another three hours laughing and talking as if we were friends for a decade or so. She asked me to run errands with her which consisted of grocery shopping, paying bills, setting her hair appointment, a yoga workout, and walking her dog Harlem. He's the cutest little yorkie I've ever seen. He's so energetic, and so friendly. I myself am not a pet lover but somehow he convinced me. Like how can you resist him he's so cute. After that she asked me what are my intentions and what did I want from her. She asked if I really wanted to be her friend or was I going to be like everyone else. This is where my heart dropped. And I chose to be a coward like you. I didn't tell her that I'm writing a book or that I'm working side by side with Elaine. I pushed hard to get to know her. It would have ruined everything. It would have also destroyed her. So I told her that I was a young woman just like her that had been hurt before and only wanted to make a real friend. I think we have a lot in common and so far it's been great being around someone that likes the same things that I do. I know I was wrong. You don't have to place your hand on your hip like that. I'm no better than you huh? I plan to make her the star of my story. Who knows maybe this could even become a series. The Cursed Series! How does that sound? It's the curse that keeps on giving. Ok now it's your turn. After hearing all of this don't you think she and Elaine should mingle one last time. I thought about asking her myself but I don't want to ruin our connection. I don't want her to think or feel that it was all just for a personal gain because it's not. I think she's a great person and I do consider her my friend now. It's just business you know," asked Tia.

"First let me say wow. You are spectacular at what you do. I have never taken that from you. We both know that's why I asked you to come join us. Second, what I do in my personal life whether right or wrong, has nothing to do with you. I don't respect blackmail. And last but not least, if she is your newfound friend, you should feel free to ask for anything. Or just as you tried to tell me... be straight forward with her. Why don't you fill her in on the plan? You see so much potential right? So mention Elaine to her and take things from there. I love all of the heartfelt moments, and I appreciate you for digging up my existence too but I still will not be a part of this. So if you thought making this huge mess and threatening my marriage would somehow convince me, try again. If my husband and I are meant to be we will move past anything that comes our way. He knows me and I know him. I am no saint and neither is he. I made a fool of myself but marriage is about being a team and working through differences. We both vowed to love each other every day through the good and bad for the rest of our lives. I'm ready to live up to my end of the deal if he is. If not then I guess I will learn a lesson but you and Elaine can forget about me helping you. So carry on with trying to use Trevor for leverage, do what you please, but I want nothing to do with you or her. As far as I'm concerned, you're both sick very sick. I recommend perhaps using some of that education towards yourself if I do say so. It's a shame to see you waste it away like this. But don't you think if Mariah wanted to get in touch with her own dear aunt that she would have already. She knows where she is. She's the reason why she's there. Why are you butting into such a toxic situation? I reckon your story would be just as lovely without badgering Mariah. I'm almost a thousand percent sure that your chicken scratch overlaps. You probably have notes for days don't you? Just from the summaries, you shared a little while ago I can tell you kept your eye on her like a hawk. So use what you have and stop this while there's still time," replied Avah.

"That's not the response that I am looking for. Time is up. I tried to help you. Now you're going to wish you didn't try me," said Tia.

Tia pulls her bun tighter before heading toward the kitchen. She demands that Elaine tie Avah's hands and feet together. She starts washing her hands and scoops three handfuls of water from the faucet to drink. She turns on the small stereo placed in the middle of the kitchen table. She starts dancing in the middle of the floor as if preparing for a boxing match. The phone begins to ring but she doesn't check it. She tells Avah and Elaine to pay it no mind as well. Then she goes back to dancing. Elaine stands up and moves far away from Avah. As she steps in the kitchen Tia jumps. She's so into the music playing that she didn't hear anyone coming behind her. Elaine seems more frightened. She's not sure what's coming next. Tia tells her that her surprise should be here in about ten minutes. Then she hugs Elaine and tells her that Avah won't get in their way. The two women share a tight squeeze hug with their eyes closed. Once opened again they're greeted with darkness as the power went out.

"Tia what is happening? Why are the lights off," asked Elaine?

"Remain composed. I'm sure one of us hit the switch by accident that's all. Just turn them back on," said Tia.

"Do you hear the flicking? That's what I am doing but it's not working. I don't think this is an accident. Double-check on Avah," replied Elaine.

"Your nerves are getting the best of you. This is totally normal. Do you see the phone over there," asked Tia.

"The phone is most likely in the same place as the power," said Elaine.

"This isn't a time for wisecracks. I'm being serious. Just grab Avah from the couch and we will go upstairs. I have flashlights up there so it'll be fine," said Tia.

"Okay, it's your show. You got it boss," said Elaine.

Elaine feels around for every object and piece of furniture in the kitchen and the living room on her way to the seat where

Avah is sitting. She tells her to get up. She doesn't hear or feel any movement so she starts using her left hand to feel on the couch. First, she touches the sides, then each seat individually. Then she removes the cushions one by one but still no Avah. She can hear Tia scrummaging through things upstairs. Her short heeled boots are tap, tapping back and forth. She's cursing in mandarin. Elaine is lost and had no clue she fluently spoke another language. She tells her it shouldn't take this long to move Avah. Elaine doesn't know what to do. She knows when she goes upstairs without Avah, Tia is going to have a holy fit. How will she explain? It doesn't seem to make sense because she was just there. Is that why the power blew out? Better yet is Avah the cause of it? Has she been one step ahead of them the whole time? These thoughts chase Elaine in a circle. Still trying not to panic, she grabs one more bag of popcorn and presses her way to the next floor of the house. At the top of the steps she nearly falls flat on her back because she almost steps on a phone. She looks down and the first thing that comes to mind is how many telephones are there in this house. It seems like when one goes missing another pops right up. They're always ringing too. She doesn't answer but instead rushes it into one of the bedrooms so Tia can hear as well. Tia pushes the talk button...

"Hello, ladies! I'm sorry about the lights. I prefer a more dim setting. I had to leave so that I can make it in time for supper. Sean is not the best cook. What kind of wife would I be if he were to starve? I know you're in a daze. This is a puzzle me escaping from the couch and all. Let's just say now we all know what we're up against. But one last thing. Before you try and sabotage me, make sure all your bases are covered. Elaine, there are four gentlemen waiting at the door to bring you back to the facility. Don't you worry I've suggested only three pills tonight, all of which will help you sleep well of course. My sweet Tia look at the opposite door. There's a detective there and an officer filled with joy. It's been brought to their attention that you've kidnapped a patient. I wonder who told them that. Now that is a chilling thriller for you. Quite ironic right? Isn't that what you're writing? Looks like you'll have some new juicy details. Now you'll have some free time to really explain what you all thought you were going to accomplish here today. Since your side probably won't hold up too well once you open that door. Well that will be all for now. I suppose we'll be speaking again soon ladies. Take care and be blessed," said Avah. The women looked at each other, defeated.

CHAPTER 4:
HER OPEN LETTER

Dear Diary,

It's me again...

As you know when I first went away, I was filled with so much animosity towards my Aunt Elaine. A lot of what actually happened has become a blur. On some occasions I can remember things right down to the very second like what I was wearing or the fact that I didn't get to see a sweet 16 like the other kids in the neighborhood. Other times I question myself and everything that I've ever known. Were my parents happy or were they both fully committed to other people outside of our household? I still hear them singing along to Let's Get It On in the Kitchen or watching Wheel of Fortune in the living room. I heard a few bad words but didn't think they were that bad. My confidence was stripped fairly early. I felt like Elaine stole what was supposed to be some of the best years of my life. I was fairly young when I learned of my aunt's twisted ways. Talk about a hidden agenda. However I was already so far gone. The manipulation and doubt was insane. She created the narrative in which I stood by. She almost switched lives with my parents swapping her union for theirs. Everything from my siblings, to my father, to even the deaths of my Aunt Spark and my Grandmother on my father's side. I doubt everything. She also formed the story behind my parent's passing. She instilled it all so often that I actually believed every word. My humble, hard working parents, hadn't the slightest clue. Well my dad might have. I remember being so small and when he and my mother would have even the tiniest disagreement, if her words got really nasty he would tell her that she sounded like her sister. He would say that if she kept going she would be alone just like her too. He didn't mean really alone like by herself because she is married. He really meant to say lonely. Her union discouraged and depressed her. But she pretended to be happy in order to compete with my mama. Isn't that sort of depressing? A man actually asked for her hand in marriage. She's never had it all together mentally from what I know now. My Daddy and everyone else except my mama could attest to it. Anybody she ever came into contact with that witnessed them together, would say just the same. My mama liked to see the good in others especially her sister so she'd totally disregard the negative comments. She wasn't the kind of woman to gossip you know? Anyway I've lived in Raleigh, North Carolina most of my life. I've attended schools, went to grocery stores, the doctors, and everything else right here in this town. I'd say it's basically all I knew then and even now. Elaine knows that and she used it to her advantage for sure. She didn't want me to know or do much. She didn't want me to get anywhere in life at all. I was in her trap stuck and helpless. But I honestly understand now that I was just the middleman needed to fulfill a much bigger plan. She didn't come up with this scenario overnight. She thought long and hard. She spent days, weeks, months, even years trying to find a solution for her disgust in my mama. This goes back before they became wives and mothers. This whole charade was personal. She could care less about me falling behind or being just another statistic because what she wanted most was coming true right before her own eyes. So what does all of this mean now? Well here I am in my mid-thirties. Physically a full grown woman, but emotionally a scarred girl trying to figure out this thing we know as life. Yesterday I dreamt I was still in the late 80's and early 90's running around playing as an innocent child should. I saw my parents smiling faces and I heard my father say that he loved me. He really did, he loved me so much. Not like the lies she pounded into my head. Today I'm holding a phone and a device called a tablet, both of which can answer anything that I think of. I can look at it and I can search any bit of news currently and ever before my time. Do you know that's how I finally found out what happened to my parents? No I don't mean the fabricated tale that all of Raleigh gloats about. I mean the whole truth, the killer, and everything else that I was forced to forget. Remember I told you I drew a blank. Well the local papers didn't and thank God for the archives as well as the ability to access them. You see some things were indeed true. I was there during the time of my parent's senseless murder. It was no accident! Elaine was there. Her Daughter Rebecca was not there, nor was her husband. Well until much later. My mama and my daddy were leaving for a work function. It was a luncheon for a promotion he was going to receive. Elaine knew this. She arrived at the house right before they planned to leave to pick me up. I was going to her house to spend some time with Rebecca. Needless to say I never made it there that day. My mama and Aunt Elaine argued about childish differences for one hour. My daddy thought she was being rude and selfish because she knew it was the day of the event. He felt like she wanted them to be late. This would leave a bad impression on his colleges. She just kept going and going and going. After each insult she stared at mama trying to see how bad she'd taken it. She refused to stop. Mama on the other hand was laughing and being so nonchalant. That triggered her even more. She pushed over our wooden shelf that holds some of our family portraits at the top row and books that Mama loved to read at the middle. The bottom shelf held trophies she won while running track in high school. A few of the items fell. She demanded that Mama stop laughing. Even then Mama only chuckled harder. She told her that if she didn't stop she'd leave me here. Mama continued and told her that it wasn't like I were a baby. I was more than capable of watching myself. That I only wanted to see Rebecca so that I wouldn't be stuck home alone and wallowing in my boredom. I started to remember everything. The shouting, the name calling, the belittling, all of it. Elaine wanted to be heard, and she wanted to matter. Mama and daddy just weren't having any of her antics. They called her a drama queen and insisted she head home. There was rage reeking from her entire soul. Her aura rang of evil. Her voice only grew louder and she refused to go home. My mama told her that she wasn't in the best state to drive so they'd call her a cab if that made her feel better. She called mama a dream killer and told her she didn't need anything from her. Then she attacked their parenting skills saying that I was incompetent and incapable of succeeding at higher levels like her daughter. I do remember now that math wasn't my best subject. In school I would get tutoring two to three times a week. My mama said that was normal. She said some people are great with English and some are great with math. She said whichever you're great in, you're probably a little less great in the other. That was totally my case. I could easily write a seventy page paper. Now ask me the square root of a number bigger than 16 and child I'd tell you that you'd know better than I would. I was thankful for those teachers and all their hard work even if they didn't get to see me finish out what we started. She left out the house and we thought she was gone. But she was still there. I recall walking upstairs to the second floor and staring at her through the window. My parents were still going out. They explained that Rebecca and I would get together another time and encouraged me to watch movies or spend some time studying. They said to disregard everything Elaine said to and about me. They said she was sick and dealing with mental illness and demons within. Mama always said that's the only reason others will try to bring you down. She said they have to be extremely upset and they don't know any other way to work through their problem than to push them on others. Daddy also said she needed to get a life. He felt mama would always excuse her lashing out like that and he could never comprehend why. He said she is an adult and needed to act like it. He said mama also needed to treat her as such and stop holding onto whatever little bit of loyalty there was between them. I kept reading through the article. It said once I woke up there I stood with Elaine, Rebecca, my uncle and my parent's lifeless bodies. Yes surprisingly they showed up right on time one would say. I guess they chose to wait until the act was completed. She came back in through the back door and made her way down into the basement. My mother and father were basically out the front door when the lights went out. Do you know I can still hear my mama telling my daddy to hold on a second as she tried flicking on the lights? My daddy replied okay but hurry. Then they both yelled out love you Mariah. Those were the last words either of them spoke. Multiple shots were fired. Then moments later a force pushed me down the stairs. My fall wasn't too hard, but I did hit my head. I was knocked out for a few and when I woke up I'd realized I had gone to hell. Everyone was gathered around me including Rebecca. I can still see her face back then. We were so young you know? She had to protect her mother. That's what I told myself. I know they're not the same and she didn't mean for me to hop from facility to facility. But she couldn't speak up or she would have been sucked into the same curse of guilt and shame right with her disturbed mother. It's like being in between a rock and a hard place. She loved her mama and she loved me too. Who really wants to see their parent in a prison or a mental institution? At least with me after bumping my head she could tell me anything and I went with it. That's how I came up with those elaborate adventures like leaving Raleigh and meeting the man of my dreams and stuff so long ago. How do you think I kept my spirits high? It was the lies that she fed me. Have you noticed yet that many of the things she said happened with my parents or myself actually happened to her? Don't you wonder why I stopped speaking? It was all because of her. She told me that I snapped and did something that I couldn't take back. She claimed me as a monster. She created a world nothing like my reality. She did everything in her power to portray me as her. That's how I see it. But again we're focusing on the positives so I'd say at the time living in that fantasy world gave me hope. She made me look crazy but I'm, thankful because everything happens just as it should. My uncle on the other hand was a perfectly capable adult. He also feared her. I imagined he couldn't tell you what it felt like to wear the pants in his own home? She always had them on. She would tell him when to breathe if she could and he'd say sure thing master. He was a puppy dog if I ever knew one. She never really loved him. He was an accessory that helped her in competing with mama. It didn't look presentable to have a baby and no husband so she held onto him. There was never any love or companionship, just Rebecca. Having sexual encounters with another man couldn't even make him grow the confidence to walk away from her. Instead they all agreed that I did it but in all actuality I never even saw the weapon until reading this article. I never touched it, but I was cursed of course. They found me to be unstable and wished me away before I had the chance to explain. I still don't really know how or why a system meant to protect could have done something so cruel so quickly. She had everyone fooled. I mean everyone from my parents, to her family, to me, to the law. We all fell victim to Elaine's devilish ways. Do you know that I'm still unlearning and learning things about myself every single day? Do you know how it feels to have complete strangers come up to you shouting and screaming while you're only trying to run simple errands or enjoy a meal? Even though the story has resurfaced again since me being free, this is my life on a regular basis. This is what I had to deal with, what I have been dealing with, and what I will probably deal with for the rest of my life. So how do I continue? Where do I find revenge? Where will my strength come from? I've learned to look for the good like my mama. If I work for the yes and totally ignore the No, I know that I can get the job done. I believe that is true with anything I'm trying to accomplish. I also know that it's okay to leave a situation without always feeling the need or obligation to explain your side...unless the opportunity really presents itself. With that being said if a person goes as far as Tia did I find it to be my duty to give her just what she needs. Would you agree? I love that you don't allow things like my thoughts to form an opinion of me. What's next may shock you. Then again, with what I've written so far, you should be fine. When Tia and I met a little while back, she was partially honest about her occupation. She did admit that she was a therapist and in a profession that aims to help people like me overcome trauma, sadness, and depression. I thought how awesome that is! She told me that she recently saw on the news what authorities did to Elaine. She said that she was sorry it took them so long to discover the actual story and that it pained her to see a young woman like myself go through such a tragic experience. She was almost sincere. It felt like she and I were becoming friends. We started meeting up almost everywhere but during each meeting I began to notice that my family was the primary topic of discussion. She chose to leave out the fact that she was working as Elaine's shrink. She also chose to leave out that she chose to work outside of their regular sessions. Lastly she chose to eliminate the tiny fact that she was working on a book about my life without hope of me ever finding out. But wait, there's more. Do you know the biggest detail she leave out? Tia Andrews forgot to let everyone know that she's Rebeca's younger sister. I'm just as stunned as you probably are. That's right, she's Elaine's second daughter that didn't make it home from the hospital. Yup she's not her God-daughter. She is her birth mother. Do you recall what I said about the perception of things? One night many years ago while my dear aunt and uncle were pretending to like each other, Elaine grew tired of the skit and decided to take an impromptu trip to New Jersey. We have lots of family in New Jersey. As kids she and mama would always stop by to see everyone. The family changed as they grew older. However while being there this particular time, she visited the prudential center for a concert. As she was dancing and snapping her fingers, wearing a mini skirt with a fitted shirt, and shaking her hips, her eyes locked with a man slightly younger than her. Her strong stare traveled down his body and back up to his left hand where she saw a ring shining bright. He matched her gaze noticing a similar feature on her left hand, and walked over to greet her. He said that his name was Parker Andrews and he was interested in seeing more of her. Shortly after they left the venue and followed each other to the Sheraton. They laughed and joked for hours. At first it seemed platonic. It was as if they both needed a listening ear but then they were reminded of those passionate stares. It turned into a night that they couldn't take back even if they tried. A month after returning home Elaine found out that she was pregnant. My pea brain of an uncle couldn't have been the father because they weren't indulging in any sexual activity during that time. From what

Rebecca remembers being that she was just a little girl herself, they were sleeping in different rooms. She said many nights she actually slept in the bed with my aunt. So when she came to him ready to spill her heart out, he wasn't mad. He only wanted answers because he suspected it went on much longer than she admitted. Without any hesitation she confessed to her night full of lust. She wasn't remorseful, ashamed, or scared that she'd lose her marriage. She still had Parker's number and his scent on the shirt she wore that evening. With his first and last name they were able to locate his work and home address. He was also only visiting New Jersey, but lived in Maryland with his wife and three children. They along with Rebecca, took a trip to Maryland to speak with him. They also told his wife everything. Surprisingly everyone had the same solution. After discovering all of their backgrounds and images that they wanted to uphold, all parties decided that it would be best for Elaine to give birth and send Tia to live with Parker and his wife as their fourth child.

My mama found out that she was carrying, but she didn't bring it up until my aunt did. Elaine gained so much weight, she was always tired, and irritable. She finally told mama that she was expecting but stress caused her to lose the baby. She said there were complications at birth that the doctors couldn't get around. When Mama asked why they chose to travel all the way to Johns Hopkins Hospital she said because they were one of the best in the country. They had this conversation in front of Rebecca. You know what they say, kids will be kids. But they should have realized that having a child around grown up conversations wouldn't always work in their favor. Tia came here and decided not to change her name because her father and mama raised her as their own. His wife Cassandra, tied her tubes after their third child. She was furious at her husband's actions, but she refused to watch Tia suffer. She still loved parker as well and wanted to work through this. It wasn't until Tia was 18 years old that they chose to tell her about Elaine. While in college as an escape from her own dysfunctional history, she chose to study the mind as a way to help others. Once they broke the news to her she started to struggle with finding her identity. That's when she knew she had to see Elaine. Then while in a psych class she learned about me. She became obsessed with the both of us. My aunt and Rebecca were both named in the specific article. Tia called a hotline listed which passed her over to three or more other sources before gaining access to Elaine. Right before graduating college, they agreed to meet. Yup you guessed it, she came right on down here to Raleigh. She went to Elaine's house and they had a meal prepared by Rebecca. You know forgiveness is a powerful tool. It's like saying I am taking back my voice and what you've done to me won't be done again! I forgave Rebecca before leaving the facility. We're back to normal. We're like the best friends that our mothers should have been. So it's only right that I told her about my friend that I was having so many great conversations and lunches with. I thought she died when I said the name. She didn't blink. She didn't speak. She just stood there. She's a pretty neutral person. She knows what her mother did to me so she understood it was in everyone's best interest to keep matters regarding either of us separate. However she knew when I said Tia's name that Elaine had something to do with us knowing one another. And do you know what? She was right! I took my time with contacting Avah because Rebecca and I had a better idea in mind.

I wonder if the officer squealed and told her that it was me who called... I mean I wouldn't be so upset either way. Since they went through such great measures I'm going to make both of their days. That's right, I'll stop by Rhythm Fit to speak with dear auntie and the precinct to chop it up with Officer Peter's. We go way back to when Elaine almost got me life you know for all of this. What are aunts for right? He said from the first day he met me he knew someone was trying to abuse their power and abuse me. He stood in my corner through everything and wrote me. He kept me uplifted in prayer, ordered me great nutritious meals, and visited every chance he got. Looks like Tia picked the wrong side to be on to me. What do you think?

Oh one last thing I almost forgot. I chose to spare Avah because I didn't know that she was cheating on Sean with my Trevor until this week. Trevor and I are done! I thought he and I had something special but that's impossible. I thought because he was in the church he would be honest but how naïve of me just to assume. I'm glad that we weren't that serious. I'm shattered just a bit but it's nothing that can't be fixed. As you know this doesn't touch what I've been through. I considered keeping my mouth shut but since Avah is into sharing all sorts of things, I'm going to spend a couple extra minutes at the center so that I can converse with her and Sean.

Until Next time,

Mariah S. Beauvoir

CHAPTER 5:
LOCK HER UP AND
THROW AWAY THE KEY

It's dark, cold, and so loud. Swear words are hopping from cell to cell. The floors creek and the smell sort of reeks as Mariah moves swiftly down the hall. There aren't any photos, not even a smiling greeter. There's only one guard and a warden with a bad attitude and a notepad. He doesn't have an ID or any kind of badge. He only points toward the way she should walk. It's so dull, so dead rather. The only hint of color she sees is gray and silver if you'd like to take the bars into account. There's nothing but women in dingy orange jumpsuits everywhere! No one has their hair done. Not one neat ponytail or a bun. Their shoes are worn down, and let's not even talk about their nails. Soap and water could really do wonders especially for their mouths. Insults fly left and right, but she keeps her head held high as she keeps walking down the path that doesn't seem to have an end. Whistle noises poke at her attention and wise remarks give her face a frown. Yet she keeps going further down the hall until she reaches cell 1990. As she stands in front of the cell, she's met by a second guard and a familiar yet tired face.

"Andrews step forward. You have a visitor here," said the guard.

"What are you doing here," asked Tia?

"Well isn't that a southern welcome. Oh yes I forget you're not actually from Raleigh. How are you? How are things going in here? It's so chilly. Do you have enough blankets? How is the book going," asked Mariah?

"Did you really come here for this? What do you want from me Mariah? I'm no longer working on the book. My lawyer feels it's in my best interest to leave you and the family alone," said Tia.

"You say the family as if you are a part. Ha! You're no better than your mother. You were really going to use me to help your sorry career. I'm not mad at you. I see it's in your DNA. I came here to warn you. I think you should take whatever deal they are offering you. I know you've only been in here for an exact week but I can tell you're not made out for this environment. You should know that it's only going to get worse. Also my lawyer found a couple interesting skeletons in your closet that he just so happened to share with yours. So let me reiterate how crucial it is that you take the deal. Next time if you'd like to write anything about me, try being upfront. You'd think with your mothers past you'd try to be better than her. She didn't raise you so I'm not sure how you two are so alike. But it's never a good idea to manipulate or use a person for your own personal gain. Especially if that person is me," said Mariah.

"What do you mean? We also tried to help you. What about Avah and Trevor? Was I not thinking about your feelings and how I knew you would feel like an idiot," asked Tia?

"No you weren't at all. You and your crooked mother were thinking about how you could blackmail Avah into a meeting with me and Elaine. Then you two also wanted to hurt me in the process if she couldn't meet your request. Keep in mind I know Elaine better than you think you do," said Mariah.

"Alright look at it this way, I was only trying to make you a star. I read somewhere that you are always focused on turning losing situations into winning ones. That's all I wanted for you. I want to make a series and you were going to be the leading role," said Tia.

"That would have been so cool except this is real life and not a movie or a book. You were trying to play with my life. You were scraping against the little bit of courage and self-esteem that I have left, and you didn't even care. Your book, movie or whatever you had in mind would have only benefited your pockets. Otherwise when we spoke during those so many lunch dates, you would have mentioned your actual intentions. This would have given me the chance to join or dismiss you from my presence. Doing things your way, eliminated that option for me. I didn't have a choice. You just went on ahead with carrying out your project," said Mariah.

"Did you come all the way here to argue with me? Do you have some sort of point or something you're looking to take away from today? Clearly we can see that you're not the only person that thinks I am wrong or I wouldn't be here right now," said Mariah.

"I am here because I feel sorry for you. I feel sorry that you felt the need to seek out a woman that never wanted you. A woman that had you and drove miles to abandon you. A woman that gave you to his flings wife and returned home to live her life with her actual family. I do not want anything from you Tia Andrews. I think you lost enough the day you decided to work in cahoots with Elaine. She is back in the institution because of the things I am saying to you. I am telling you from my own knowledge. I know how convincing she can be. She seems like she means well at first. Then you end up well you end up like how you are right now. And what can she do for you now? How is she going to get you out of this? What about all your hard work? What about your degree? What about your licenses?

You've put everything that you worked so hard for at risk. And it's not even like you can hide any of it. The articles on me were there, but I know you searched. The internet, the phones, the computers today have everything. With a click of a mouse I can tell you who you are without you saying one word," said Mariah.

"So basically you're asking me to give up the relationship that I've made with my mother? You should understand what I'm dealing with. You know better than anyone else how it feels to do without being that your parents are dead. I always knew there was something different about me. I didn't have my mother all along. What we've been able to establish, has been the biggest blessing of my life. I know she's not perfect, and I know she's made mistakes, but I will love her imperfect and all. Avah and I were once really great friends. I had to lose her to save my mother so that should show where my loyalty lies,' said Tia.

"But she is in a health center where they will cater to her needs. You are in here where they could give a damn. Do you understand that you are in trouble? Why won't you let me help you," asked Mariah?

"I believe you should first help yourself. You know I read something somewhere that your mother was worth a fortune. That must have come in handy with all that happened. I bet it was even better being an only child," said Tia.

"Excuse me? What are you asking me," asked Mariah.

"Oh nothing at all. I'm just bringing to light something that I observed that's all. I guess I'm saying despite what my mom did either you've already been awarded or will be awarded a nice lump pretty soon. Am I right," asked Tia?

"I spent a fair portion of my life being bounced around from crazy home to crazy home. I lost both my parents, I have no kids...I have nothing. My mother made sure that before she went on home to be with the lord that should anything ever happen to her, I'd be okay. Is it okay that I'm at least financially stable? Can I have that," asked Mariah?

"And you've known that all along right? Your mother didn't just tell you one day out of the blue. You didn't just find out a year or so ago or while being admitted to any of the institutions. Is it possible that you and my mother discussed this? Did my mother tell you? Is it possible that you're only telling some of the truth just like my mother? Maybe she did pull the trigger but maybe you wanted her to. At 15 years old you certainly know right from wrong right? Maybe my mother knew when you turned 25 you'd receive all of this money and you would be set for the rest of your life. She explained how life would be grand. But then she betrayed you. You did a few extra years in various facilities and the extra drama you two are currently working through. But before then you all had a clear thought out plan. Isn't that possible," asked Tia?

"Wo you really are an author. That was brilliant if I do say so myself. I'm still not so sure why she chose to include you. Guard I'm ready to go now. Ms. Andrews here seems to be a little touched or something," said Mariah.

"What? Answer me! It's true isn't it? You knew! You knew the entire time. You wanted her to do it. There's nothing wrong with you. You were pretending. You're a fake! They gave you food, kept a roof over your head, and now you're rich! You ungrateful brat. My mother isn't sick you're sick. And she included me because she didn't trust you. I figured you out…and that bothers you," said Tia.

"You have no idea…take care of yourself in here Tia. I hear the winter's get very very cold. You've been quite entertaining but I should be going now," said Mariah.

Mariah buttons her long trench coat and wraps her scarf around her neck. Then a guard comes right over to assist her toward the other end of the prison. Tia voice sings miserably as Mariah's high heels click clack across the titled floor. The guard looks at her and she tells him that her little cousin is struggling with a lot these days. He nods his head and the two of them keep on walking. When they get to the main entrance she sees Officer Peters sitting at a desk. She stops right in front of him and he offers her a seat. Coincidentally it's his 40th birthday today. When he met Mariah He was 19 and she was 15. It was his second year on the force, and he'd just lost his little sister in a house fire. She was only 12 years old so that's why she and her case stood out to him. He felt like he owed it to his sister to take care of her in any way that he could. Although he wasn't much older the difference at that time was significant. He saw her as his second chance. She was the right to his wrong.

"Well hello there beautiful. What can I do for you today," asked Officer Peters?

"Hey Handsome birthday boy. How are you feeling today? It's all about you. I don't need anything at the moment. I just finished speaking to my estranged cousin Tia. She still doesn't seem like she's going to cooperate. I'm trying to do everything in my power to help her but she has some imagination you know," asked Mariah?

"So I've heard. I was out two nights ago with a couple of the fellas at StarDunkin over on Woodbridge Ave getting coffee and donuts and you all came up. Apparently she was involved with one of the rookie cops. His name is Julian Jameson. He's from up north over in some town called Rahway. I hear it's out of New Jersey, but I'm not really familiar. Anyway he just relocated because his girlfriend Taylor McFall got accepted into North Carolina Central University with a full ride scholarship. She's studying for her Master's. When I heard her name I got really quiet because it doesn't sound like Tia to me. So it was about an hour into us hanging out and he arrives. The first thing I did was pull him to the side and ask about both girls. Do you know he confirmed it? He didn't lie not even a bit. He said yes Taylor is my girlfriend and so is Tia," said Officer Peter's.

"Well what a bold man. I can't say that I'm surprised. Some people lack morals. I wonder if she knows. Being that she's a product of my aunt. I'd bet she does. I would also bet that she doesn't even care. Poor Taylor... although I don't know her, she sounds lovely. She has a good head on her shoulders but of course that's never enough for some people. A thrill is all they're after. Chasing to be chased meanwhile missing out on an authentic catch," said Mariah.

"I agree some individuals don't realize when they have a good thing right in front of them. But thank God that's not the case for all of us right," asked Officer Peters?

"Absolutely. Oh tell Trevor I said thank you for his help. It worked out great. They totally thought he and I were a legit thing. Isn't that hilarious," said Mariah.

"Trev is the best. He's been one of my closest friends since we pledged together at Winston-Salem State University. You know outside of the Police Department he's also an actor. He was thrilled to work with us. Tia should have researched a little more," said Officer Peters.

"That's what happens when you don't have your facts straight. Maybe her stay here will give her some time to educate herself. That way the next time she tries to come she's prepared for what I'll send her way in return. But let's not focus on that. Today is all about you. When you finish your shift you should meet me at the house. I have something I'd like to give you,' said Mariah.

"I always love your surprises. Ok I will head straight home from here. Oh and one more thing Mariah. I am so proud of you and all of your growth. I told you to be patient. I told you you would have your freedom and things would work out. Look at you now, and look at those who hurt you. I'm just delighted to be here with you taking it all in. You are absolutely amazing to me. You always have been… I love you," said Officer Peter's.

"You've been the most consistent person in my life. You never judged me even when I opened up every ugly scar to you. You are mine and I'm yours forever my dear. We're almost finished with what we started. I love you more. I wish Elaine would have followed simple directions like you did. But one thing my mama told me as a little girl, you can't take everyone to that next level with you no matter how bad you may want to. Lord knows I tried but at least she's getting proper care now," said Mariah.

"Your mama was intelligent. I have to say I agree with her. I still think you're too kind for the way in which you view Elaine. I know in my heart of hearts that she was using you. But I know your heart. It's so pure you'd never even see it coming. But you're right about one thing. Rhythm Fitness is the best company in all of Raleigh especially since Avah doesn't want Sean to know about our dear friend

Trevor. I hear she's been keeping a strict eye on Elaine. You have nothing to worry about," said Officer Peters.

"And that keeps my heart at ease. Well I should be going. One more thing, before you leave just make one more round and check in on Tia. If things are really playing out the way she wrote in this manuscript, she's going to need lots of attention. Thank you again for confiscating it. It's a crying shame I'll have to be the one to finish it. But I won't lie I'll always be a little curious as to what her ending would have been. She really wanted Elaine and I to catch up. Do you think Elaine guaranteed something? Do you think she made some sort of promise? What were they going to do to me if we did meet up? All of these questions we'll probably never have the answers to….oh well. Also before I forget you have to be the one to do the check. Don't send any of the other cops on duty. She will have them wrapped around her finger. We have to always keep in mind that she's still a trained specialist herself," said Mariah.

"Your beauty keeps me at ease. Look at that pencil skirt. Gray is your color. And that blouse looks incredible. Your shoes are stunning almost just as much as you are. Don't think I didn't' notice your hair cut either. You are so beautiful. I am a lucky man. Don't shy away either. I mean every word Mariah. But yes I will make sure she's okay. As far as their intentions, I always thought Elaine had a dream of her own. You were always just her little helper. She planned to exploit you any way possible because that's what she wanted to do to your mother. Elaine wanted nothing more than to be better than Evelyn. When she noticed it wasn't possible she chose to go deeper. Tia just like you got hit in the crossfire. Kidnapping is a very serious crime and since she chose not to discuss her mother's involvement and most likely will deny the plea, she's going to spend many long nights staring at those same walls. But the choice is hers. I doubt that Elaine made any extravagant advances or promises. Just imagine having the opportunity to have a relationship with the person you've longed to see or be around for so long. She wanted Elaine in her life. She wanted to break through her own demons in finding her true identity. She wanted to relate, to feel loved, and most importantly to understand you. You can't knock her for having ambition. She got so close," said Officer Peters.

"She didn't succeed because she wasn't a part of the original plan. Mommy dearest manipulated her and set her up for failure. Whatever relationship they were working on could have been established without trying to remake my story. She wants to be an author. And that's another thing, shouldn't that be a flag for Elaine?

I would question that. Is she actually trying to form a bond, or is she forming a bond to launch her career as a published author," asked Mariah?

"I'd say it could be either scenario. You would think of the career because you're not one that is going to trust others so easily no matter who they are. But someone else might think it just so happened that she's a great writer and used her skills as a way to cope with the recent obstacles she's been facing. It all depends on how you look at it babe," said Officer Peters.

"True...you have a point. We will leave it at that. I know you have things to do so you can get out of here early enough to enjoy the rest of your day. I don't want to talk your ears off all through the evening. Well not about any of this. Thank you again for everything. I will see you later on tonight. I have one more stop, but I'll be home right after that," said Mariah.

"You're heading over to Rhythm Fit aren't you," asked Officer Peters?

Mariah chooses not to answer Officer Peters. Instead she walks around to the back of his desk placing her hands around his neck. She leans in lower using the strength of her calf muscles to hold her up. Then she gives him the sweetest peck on the cheek and pats his soft sandy hair before placing his hat on his head. As she stands back up she gathers her skirt and puts her hair up into a low bun. Then she struts her stuff side to side showing off her hips and that million dollar smile that she never hides. After that she grabs her purse that's filled with everything she should ever need in life, her car keys, the manuscript, and Officer Peters Hand. A few of the other officers are storming back in from lunch so she gives his hand a firm shake, thanks him for his services, and turns toward the exit. He smiles as he watches her walk away. From his window he can see her walking to her car and looking into her rearview mirror. She can see him too. He starts to laugh, taps his desk, hums a tune, and gets his belongings together as well. She starts her car up, adjusts her mirror, and gives one last wink as she drives to the stoplight.

CHAPTER 6:
TIME TO TAKE THE
MASK OFF

The tired sun creeps through the windows of the Rhythm Fitness facility striking the faces and bodies of patients and staff members. Each door opens wide as the nurses' swarm in, to hand out medicine and breakfast. It's 6:30 p.m. which means it's time for evening inspections. Everyone's on the floor attending to the needs of the most important people in the building. Medicines, snacks, sheets, and laundry skip from room to room. Pens scribble against clipboards checking off attendance and servings. It's a pretty nice Monday but nothing out of the ordinary. Cups of apple juice and orange juice accompany each meal and two sugar cookies top it off. It's been a week since Avah was so blessed to have broken away from the wrath of Elaine and Tia. Since then she and Sean have made lots of changes within the building and the company's policies as a whole. He's still clueless about Trevor but happy about the recent glow and change in his wife's behavior. He recently told her that he's not so sure what had gotten into her but he knew one thig for sure...it was definitely helping her performance within their businesses. Elaine on the other hand has been placed on 24-hour watch. She has one on one attention around the clock. She isn't allowed to do or go anywhere alone. Everyone knows to keep a look out just in case she tries to make a run for it.

Don't let her steal the show, there are still so many new changes. Like the fact that all of the walls in the rooms have been painted sky blue as a calming mechanism. Visiting hours have been reduced throughout the week, and there's a new alarm system to match the sliding doors. Should any patient try to leave the premises, a light shock goes to each of the employees through their new wrist watches. Scrubs are to be worn at all times. There's no longer any dress down Fridays. There's no grace period either, late is late and there's no debate! There's a bunch of touch devices. Each patient is scanned via face recognition when going in and out of their rooms. As a conflict of interest if a family member is already checked in, a nurse of relation cannot be hired to care for them. There's no such thing as a favorite. All guest are loved equally. Floors are mopped three times a day now and waxed every Wednesday and Friday. Breaks are only thirty minutes long and two call outs results in possible suspension. Each room has a new book shelf filled with great literature. Reading periods are required two times a day. Television use is minimalized. There will be no programs that display violence and or vulgar language. Swearing is prohibited. Every second Saturday is dedicated to Bingo night. The winner gets an extra half hour of television or a special treat from the kitchen. Most likely it'll be sugar free jello or a banana. Diet awareness is very important. You are what you eat and the staff of Rhythm Fit will always practice what they preach.

All of these fantastic changes are in accommodation to Mariah. Just two days after the kidnapping incident, Mariah called and spoke to Avah. Before expressing her happiness about her safe return in a sarcastic way of course, she let her know that she was aware of her involvement with Trevor. She also thanked her for having a little bit of backbone despite having no integrity. Mariah appreciated Avah for refusing to set her up with meeting Elaine against her wishes. She told her that she didn't approve of Tia and Elaine's actions, but she applauded her for going against the grain because she knew that they planned on crumbling up her marriage, yet she still made the right decision. But in the same breath she told her that she didn't agree with infidelity and that she was a piece of crap for screwing around on Sean. Then to add icing to the cake Mariah still decided to do just as they did unless Avah agreed to her terms. Although distraught, Avah knew she had no choice. Plus, Mariah's demands weren't half as bad as Tia's. The only thing Avah didn't know is that Mariah really wouldn't have been bothered if she and Elaine were to meet up. She was still in the dark about everything. With Tia in prison and Elaine is in the looney bin, Mariah is left living happily.

The same heels that tapped through the prison began tapping in the next room over from Elaine. Her ear is glued to the wall. In one hand she has a stress ball, and in the other she has a pocket-sized calendar with multiple dates checked off. Her left hand starts to shake and her right legs leans almost as if she's going to fall. She's not steady. She knows that walk anywhere. She knows the scent too. Her handshakes a little more and a picture of Mariah falls from the booklet. It's an oldie but goodie you know like when she was five or six. In the visual Elaine is holding her hand and they're at what possibly looks like an amusement park. Her mother nor Rebecca are pictured. Her eyes start to swell but she snatches the tears back in. She looks at her bed and the gown the nurses have chosen for her to wear today and she throws it on the floor. Then she kicks off her shoes and replaces them with slipper socks. She tiptoes closer to the door still listening to Mariah's shoes dancing away. She's supposed to be sleep but she's fighting it. She always fights her sleep. Her therapist says it's because she obsessed and has lost track of reality.

Most days consists of crying and overanalyzing the past. She talks about Mariah and some pact more than anything else. She keeps saying that someone made a mistake and they're wrong for having her in the center. She talks about her daughter from time to time as well. She hasn't visited yet. One of the assistants reached out over the weekend but she said she still didn't think that Elaine was settled enough. She said she doesn't want to be in the way or make any extra added work. That's what most families say when they've decided to cut their love ones loose. They tend to look for excuses but never a solution that could make their relative feel better you know like actually visiting them. There's another voice interrupting her peace of mind. She's unable to make out most of their words, but she hears him asking about her background and history. It's likely he's trying to get to know her. The shoes pause but Mariah's giggles don't.

You'd think she were a comedian. Elaine thinks her flirt laugh is dry but she's still peeking and waiting. She's waiting for the first chance she gets to introduce Mariah to the back of her hand should she fearlessly walk into her room. She's getting closer. The laugh is calming down but the heels are still shuffling away. She's almost there. She's so close that if she were to extend her hand she'd surely touch the knob. Elaine can't take it! She moves directly in front of the door where she can feel Mariah on the other side. Giggling continues to invade the premises and a raspy tone gets on the loud speaker. It's a special message from Avah. She wants everyone to know that Mariah is there to visit and if anyone would like some company that she's more than happy to spend some time. The stress ball bursts in Elaine's hand because she can't understand why Avah is treating her like some sort of celebrity.

She walks to her bed and sits down. She gets back up almost as soon as her behind touches the edge. She goes in the almost invisible bathroom to wash her face. She takes much longer than normal and goes over her eyes two extra times. She dips her head down and places her hands behind her head. Then she brushes her teeth and puts on her earrings. She's not supposed to have them. In most cases they're always removed from patients as a safety precaution but she's been known to raise sand. Even with being stuck in the room she still manages to scare Avah a bit. She's the one that informed the nurses to overlook it. Two have bombarded her so far and she simply replies that Elaine is an older woman stuck in olden times and if they try to change too much about her she'll show them how sour the south can get. Most of the nurses are younger millennials. Elaine hates that too. She says they can't function without some sort of technology. She told Avah right to her face that she knows for certain that's why she's so stupid and the only reason she could have possibly risked a gentleman like Sean. That was the same day she was admitted so it could have been the happy drugs talking too. They sure didn't keep her jolly for more than two hours. Once they started wearing off she began carving Tia's name in the new wooden desk that Sean just ordered. He had cleaning duty a few nights ago and had the biggest tantrum when he came across it. Fifteen minutes seems like an eternity. She knows Mariah's standing there but she's not so sure why she hasn't come in yet. She finally storms out the bathroom and plops down on her bed. Under her pillow she grabs the latest issue of Ebony Ivory Magazine and flips through the pages. Her place marker stops at page twelve. Journalist Paige Amanda wrote about a four hour coffee date she and Mariah had. Before concluding the date she told Paige that she'd found her calling in life and would be pursuing a career in writing. She said something along the lines about notes and credited prior conversations with Tia Andrews. That most likely meant she kept Tia's manuscript and plans on spicing it up since Tia's spending nights in the big house. With her stubborn ways she'll be there longer than anticipated. Elaine's just mad she didn't think of it herself. Mariah beat her to the punch yet again. Her minds racing wondering if she's here just to rub it in. Why hasn't she opened the door yet? Is she out there gossiping and snickering at her. What's so funny? Who is so funny? Elaine sits up and shoves the pamphlet back under her pillow. Then she looks at the clock. It says 6:30. She picks it up and looks underneath as if it would tell her morning or night. Then she stands up from her bed and searches under her pillow again.

The magazine is still there. She looks at it again in search of a clue. Then it dawns on her to check the year of publication. She's for certain that it's 2016 and she's only been held for a week. As she turns the booklet to the side she nearly dies. The year reads 2020. Elaine Goes Ballistic. Pages are flying everywhere! She's ripping them all out. Clothes and hangers are flying too. Shoes are banging against the door, and you can hear the bed being pushed against the wall. Screaming is an understatement. It sounds like a wrestling match is taking place. Nurses seem scared walking past. Then in the distance at the other end of the hall they see Mariah and totally disregard her cries.

"Oh my gosh it's Mariah! Wow you look even prettier than on the television and the blogs. Your hair is to die for. You don't look a day over 21. Are these your sisters? You know that's your aunt again fussing down the hall? It's been a while since you're last visit. You know if you don't come frequently she creates these fantasies. It's getting really hard to talk her off the ledge you know," asked Nurse Caldwell?

"That was a mouthful. You must be new or my aunt's behavior wouldn't ruffle your feathers much at all. Thank you for the compliment. Why, has she been lying about my age again? She keeps telling people that I'm in my mid-thirties or thirty something and that my birthday is in March. Where she got that from I'm not so sure. But that's why it's never too clear. I'm 29. My birthday is October 10, 1990. And yes you're right it has been a while because I've been on tour. I'm working on my second play and my fourth book. These beautiful ladies aren't my biological sisters, however we pledged together at The University of Maryland Eastern Shore. Meet Dr. Morgan Karma Garcia, Nurse Rebecca

Townsend, Model Tia Andrews, and Teacher Kennedy Davenport," said Mariah.

"Wait a minute I know you guys. We all do. You're right I'm new but she's had the chance to talk my ear off already. Isn't Rebecca her daughter? She talks about her and they have the same last name. Tia as well? She told us about this one wild night that resulted in a beautiful baby girl," said Nurse Caldwell.

"And the other staff members didn't tell you? My aunt is here with you all because she had a nervous breakdown and no longer can differentiate between reality and the thoughts that fill her mind. What about my family? Have you spoken to my mother or father yet? My mother is Evelyn. She was here two weeks ago. Have you been here that long? Townsend is a common name, but Rebecca isn't related to Elaine. Neither is Tia. As exciting as it sounds there wasn't any spontaneous night. My aunt was born and has lived in Raleigh, North Carolina, her whole life. The story about Kennedy is absolutely fake too. She looks super young but she's actually 25. The only person I'm related to is Avah. She's my cousin. My aunt Elaine blames her for being here. We all know that's not the case, but because of her theory she tells a nasty story about Avah. Did you hear about it? It's the one about her and Trevor Neverson? Trevor is my husband of two years now. My parents are very happy and married for 30 years now. My father is a construction worker and a plumber. He worked six nights a week to put me through school since I only got a partial scholarship. I've been writing for Ebony Ivory Magazine for 6 years now. I came here once a few years back and she attacked me. She actually tried to have me admitted. Thank God I still carry around my college ID on top of my license and that Avah was here of course to set the record straight. She came up with a lie about insurance money and my parents dying. Child it was all such a big mess. None of it was true not the schemes, the drama, the murders, not anything she's ever mentioned. Listen I never went to any facility. I graduated at 17, took a year off, and made my way to college. While in college I started writing for multiple brands. Then someone from Ebony Ivory reached out to me and I couldn't turn them down. They're one of my favorite publications. This month we have an edition called future self. We're writing about goals and desires for 2020. I wrote that I hope to write two new books and find a solution for my aunt. No one knows what she goes through, the trouble she's caused, the doubt she's created, but she's still my aunt. And I love her you know? It's been a while because it can be hard trying to be a figure in the spotlight. Blogs jump at her stories all the time because why would someone so close to you lie the way she does right? I know she can't help it but if I hadn't spoken to you as I am right now, you would know right? I forgive her because I know it all stems from much deeper issues that she nor I have any control over," said Mariah.

"Wow, you're nothing like I thought you would be and neither is your side of the curse. I don't know what to say. I'm still not so sure why she'd go that far to make you all seem like the opposite and why would she include your friends as well. It just seems like a lot of effort," said Nurse Caldwell.

"I tried solving her mystery numerous times. My feelings would get hurt wondering why my aunt would think and feel the way she does about her own family. What is this curse, and where did it come from? I would ask her that all the time. My mother finally told me that when they were little girls my aunt felt like she was treated poorly. So I asked my mother well was she? She said even then that Elaine's outlook on things was different from everyone else's. She said that she needed help but my grandparents took things lightly. They thought she'd grow out of it so they didn't push her. Well she continued to go about things the best way she knew how. One lie led to another and another, and they always grew bigger than the last. Then she started to feed those lies to me. The problem is I shouldn't have eaten them. She knows my friends because they've been around for some time now. This isn't their first time visiting. A lot of my stories are about things I've actually been through. But there are some stories that I do include my aunt's fantasies. I know it seems weird right? I'm taking some horrible and disturbing accusations and trying to find art in them. But I only do it to defeat the odds as well as the blogs. You can't hurt me if I throw it back at you right? That's why some people still find her reasoning behind her tantrums suitable. I guess they think I'm making a mockery of her so maybe I am hiding something. However, I'm really thinking my life has been pretty typical and boring but my aunt makes my life sound like something you'd see on a soap opera. There's really nothing too special. I'm the only child. My parents gave and still try to give me the world. My husband is a man of God and a surgeon. I'm working on my master's, books, and plays. I love going to the gym, smoothies, pizza, and scary movies. I have a dog named Compton, outside of work the girls and I go hiking, sailing, vacations, and bowling. Sounds pretty regular to me don't you think? But we've held you long enough from the others that I'm sure could use your assistance. Let us go on in here and check on her," said Mariah.

"I have no words. I'm just wowed is all I can say. It's been a real pleasure speaking with you. But yes you're right. I should make my rounds. The sun is almost in hiding and that's when the night changes around here. I wish you all luck with everything. Keep up the great work. Despite everything I know it doesn't seem like it at times, but she is proud of you. You don't create stories like that about someone you don't care for. I'm glad you've found a way to turn her frowns upside down," said Nurse Caldwell.

Mariah and the girls all leave Nurse Caldwell with a pleasant smile. As she walks down the hall she pauses for a second and slowly looks back but they're no longer there. They've walked toward Elaine's room and finally step inside.

"Mariah is that you? I knew you would come soon. I prayed you would come.

And you brought the girls. Hello girls how are you," asked Elaine?

"Hello Mom. I hear you've been talking a lot to a new nurse. She tells me you've been mixing things up again too. I tried to explain your condition to her but I'm not so sure how much she really took in. She seems like the kind of person that knows there's three sides to a story. Our stories are so different I'm sure. You know with everything you've said lately," said Mariah?

"Did you tell her that I'm your mother? Did you tell her what Elaine did? Does she know we're identical twins? Oh please Mariah tell me you told her. Listen I know my lifestyle didn't match your standards. But things are different now. I'm ready to come home. Elaine can go home and things can go back to the way they used to be. Your father and I can work things out. We can all go back. We can make this right," said Evelyn.

"See that's the thing Mom I'm inspired having you here. How do you think I keep coming up with these psychotic novels? You being here has become a part of my inspiration. You should have done what you needed to do before we got to this place. I don't know Aunt Elaine plays you pretty well. And you play her just as good. I told you I wanted to explore the world and go to the best schools for the profession I had in mind. You didn't want to move right then and there so I really feel like you were being selfish. So why should I be considerate now. Plus, if a change was needed Elaine could have switched with you long ago. She does work here you know. Well you work here but she's you so the same thing. You get my point right," asked Mariah?

"You sound like a spoiled child. I worked my life away to give you everything. We made do with what we had. Although it was never a lot, we were fine. Your father and I have always worked hard for you. You're holding a grudge and using me at the same time. This won't go on forever Mariah. Someone will catch on sooner or later. I don't belong here; I don't belong here. They have the wrong sister. Your aunt needs to be here so she can get the proper care. There isn't much wrong it's just a little assistance. These people can give her one on one attention. But instead you have her pretending to be a nurse. And look at these girls you've brainwashed them all. All of you so quick to sell your souls for fame. You should be ashamed. Don't you see what she's doing to her own mother? As soon as you try another way aside from hers, you will see. And don't realize Mariah? They're not your real friends?" asked Evelyn.

"Fake friends come with the career. Aunt Elaine helped me go after what I want. She knows I have the skills and abilities to write my butt off. I just couldn't find my point of interest, my target demographic and my voice. I'm so used to always telling the truth that my fake life almost has the chance to haunt me. Good thing Elaine taught me a trick for that too. She said always remember we're trying to get to Hollywood Not Heaven. That's where you messed up mom. If you only knew your role and the goal. If only you played your part. But you've still contributed, by giving me some of the best lines... I don't belong here; I don't belong here. It's not me! They have the wrong sister...Ah I actually like that ending better mom. Please keep going! Bottom line is no one wants to hear about the perfect family that stayed perfect. That's boring! You and dad were boring. Elaine is too, but she agreed and helped me find a way to build excitement. Now I have books and movie deals flying everywhere.